STARK COUNTY DISTRICT LIBRARY

3 1333 00760 4000

T5-CVJ-807

DISCARDED

JAC   F THO

Thomas, Martha Lou.

The war hero's wife

BOOK SALE

**STARK COUNTY
DISTRICT LIBRARY**
CANTON, OHIO 44702

JACKSON TOWNSHIP
BRANCH LIBRARY

THE WAR HERO'S WIFE

Also By Martha Lou Thomas

Waltz with a Stranger

The War Hero's Wife

Martha Lou Thomas

Walker and Company
New York

*To the memory of David, one of war's victims . . .
and to Dee, one of life's triumphs.*

Copyright © 1988 by Martha Lou Thomas

All rights reserved. No part of this book may be reproduced or transmitted
in any form or by any means, electronic or mechanical, including photocopy-
ing, recording, or by any information storage and retrieval system, without
permission in writing from the Publisher.

All the characters and events portrayed in this story are fictitious.

First published in the United States of America in 1988 by the Walker
Publishing Company, Inc.

Published simultaneously in Canada by Thomas Allen & Son Canada,
Limited, Markham, Ontario.

Library of Congress Cataloging-in-Publication Data
Thomas, Martha Lou.
  The war hero's wife / Martha Lou Thomas.
    p.   cm.
  ISBN 0-8027-1042-5
  I. Title.
PS3570.H5737W33 1988   88-9644
813'.54--dc19   CIP

Printed in the United States of America
10 9 8 7 6 5 4 3 2 1

Mid-June

=1=

Applause exploded along the gleaming rows of banquet guests come to honour Edward Bleddem Smith's recent successful tactics in battle, though he was making an absolute cake of himself tonight. Under the flare of flambeaux lighting the ancient hall, the realm's latest hero-come-home-from-the-war did nothing to conceal his passionate interest in the plump nymph seated across from him, despite his wife's presence at his side. Many were wagering the unlikely pair would disappear under the table before the evening's celebration was much older.

In the untenable position to the right of her husband, Lady Sarah Smith (née Davess) could only hold fast to what she hoped was a gracious smile and cling to an anger that kept nausea at bay. What if she were to stand at this moment and upend a bottle of wine atop Edward's distinguished blond head? She envisioned the liquid spilling across the aurora borealis of medals and ribbons on his well-cut uniform, and took a certain perverse pleasure from the thought. As for that creature in green satin across the table, a good drenching might cool her quivering ardour.

The applause died, and the Lord Mayor of London continued his speech. "Our eventual triumph over Napoleon's evil ambitions can be assured when such men as this lead us to victory!"

Bleddem Smith nodded to acknowledge each ringing tribute to his prowess in Mar's arena. Yet his gaze never wavered from the voluptuous Miss Aimée Orr, whose hazel eyes glowed with adoration.

Lady Sarah observed the two of them. The rumours from abroad that had plagued her since early spring were proving true. Too true. She should have ignored his orders and joined him when first the stories surfaced. Stories she had not believed.

Elegant in misty green muslin, she shuddered involuntarily and stroked the smooth moonstones in her necklace, Edward's wedding gift ten years before. Where was the officer from the auspicious day who had solemnly vowed, forsaking all others, to pursue his dream with her? Now, at this pinnacle, he shared the savouring of it with another.

The Lord Mayor's oratory reached its climax. "Gratefully, we present this sword as a symbol of our everlasting esteem."

Edward Bleddem Smith stood to accept the diamond-studded weapon. Uncharacteristically dramatic, he brandished it above his head. "To victory," he cried.

The guests rose to respond, led by the satin-draped voluptuary, sending their cheers to crash against his six feet of splendid heroism. Lady Sarah's applause merged into the whole. Tears, which had glistened in her grey eyes during the evening's ordeal, now trailed down the beautifully proportioned planes of her oval face. Whether they were tears of pride or pain or both, she did not know.

She looked down the table to her father-in-law's beaming face, then turned back, irresistibly drawn by Aimée Orr's flamboyant performance. Auburn curls artfully tousled, Miss Orr was the last to sit down, still clapping until Edward signaled her to stop. In the folds of vivid green across her capacious bosom nested a large diamond brooch. Was it from Edward? It seemed to match his present glitter.

"Distinguished company," the hero began, reverting to a monotone more suitable for explaining enemy positions than inspiring worship. "All I ask is to serve my king and my country with honour."

Honour? Lady Sarah wanted to shout in defiance. Only in war, evidently, could one rely on Edward's honour. Disillusionment threatened her fragile composure. Where was his honour tonight? And who were these . . . these adventurers who had arrived with him, and seemed so entrenched in his life? She glanced at Osmond Orr, seated just beyond his daughter and listening just as raptly to Edward's every word. My man of affairs, Edward had announced. How very appropriate. Lady Sarah added irony to her defence arsenal. Did Mr. Orr then manage his daughter's rapprochement with Edward?

"In accepting this sword, I pledge my continuing devotion . . . "

For all she pondered, Lady Sarah produced no answers. Only Edward would provide those, but she had not been alone with her husband since his return to England. The loving reunion she had so long anticipated appeared to be a casualty of war. And their marriage—was it another? Her slender fingers traced the delicate pattern of silver filigree in which her moonstones were set—so pale a light when compared to the brilliance of diamonds.

"Ain't this a happy circumstance, our own *ménage à cinq*?" asked Aimée Orr, settled in the comfortable sitting-room of the accommodations Lady Sarah had secured earlier in the week.

Another in the series of chuckles that periodically rumbled from Osmond Orr's heavy chest signalled approval. His rotund physique evoked wrestlers past their prime, working country fairs.

From a comfortable depression in the sofa's down pillow seat, the Reverend Mr. Featherstone Smith (retired) still twitched with excitement over the ride from the banqueting hall. Jubilant citizens had pulled their open carriage all the way to the hotel in Kings Street, St. James, and every inch of the cleric's small frame delighted in the homage his son inspired.

"Ned! Oh, that your mother had lived to witness this night!"

Bleddem Smith, at the tall window, did not deign to comment, but watched the crowd of his admirers dispersing. At Lady Sarah's approach, he moved away, leaving her in sole possession of his vantage point.

"Come, *mon brave*. Come away from the window to hear the newest verses of my epic poem." Aimée tapped the French armchair next to her to indicate where she wanted the hero positioned. "Lady Sarah," she prompted.

Buried in dissembling, Lady Sarah heeded the inamorata's call as complaisantly as her husband. She turned from the window, her stance poised, her slender figure enhanced by her gown's soft drape. No sign of distress marred the delicate features of her face. Only the faint tan of her complexion and the sun-washed streak that lightened her brown hair from temple to chignon hinted at the unconventional.

"I believe you have my handkerchief in your pocket, *mon brave*," Miss Orr reminded the hero. Cradling it in her hand, she arose to strike a regal pose in front of the fireplace.

"I have put my verses to music," she explained, "so common people who can't read will be able to sing about the victory. We want it remembered through the ages."

Satisfied that all eyes were on her, she crossed her hands over her breast and began.

> Our noble Edward's brow is creased,
> From war's confusion there's no surcease.
> The cannon's roar, the blood and gore,
> Splattered on the clothes he wore.

But no one worries through the fracas,
For this brave man'll not forsake us.

"She is singing flat, Sarah." The Reverend Mr. Smith turned his head to comment loudly to his daughter-in-law, still standing by the window and outside the close circle of Aimée's audience. Bleddem Smith frowned at his father before returning his full concentration to the performance.

Featherstone would not be stilled. "We need Mrs. Sparrow's voice." He turned to explain to Osmond Orr. "Used to be in our choir. Voice a bit reedy, but she could carry the tune when the others lost it." He glanced back at Lady Sarah. "Do you remember her, Sarah?"

"Perhaps she was before I came into the family, Father." Lady Sarah left the window to lay her hand lightly on his shoulder. He was wont to recall more readily the distant past than the day before yesterday.

He reached to pat her fingers. Sarah was good to him, explaining what he forgot.

"Ned, you knew Mrs. Sparrow," he insisted, his white hair a halo separating speckled bald pate from an almost cherubic face filled with the eagerness of a small boy. It was difficult to imagine him as sire to one of such heroic stature as Edward Bleddem Smith, who more nearly resembled his deceased mother's Saxon forebears.

"Yes, Father," his son responded impatiently. "I remember her, but rather than reminisce, I prefer to listen to the rest of Miss Orr's recitation with music. If you would pay closer attention, you would realise what a fine singing voice she has." The cold tone of command stilled his father.

Lady Sarah kept her hand on the chastened clergyman's shoulder.

"I know flat when I hear it," he muttered.

Undeterred, Aimée embarked once more upon the rough seas of creative effort, where treacherous shoals of criticism could shipwreck even the greatest talent.

> Oh, war is cruel, we all agree,
> And from its horrours many flee.
> But not our Edward Bleddem Smith,
> Whose courage is like a monolith.

She paused to comment, "I was particularly pleased at my rhyme for Smith. Not easy to find one, you know. What do you think, *mon brave?*"

Mon brave nodded rather than disturb the expression of benign tolerance he felt appropriate for one so honoured, then relented to praise her. "Very clever."

Aimée queried her father. "O.O., what do you think?"

Osmond Orr chuckled and raised pudgy fingers softly clapping. "You always were, my dear. Clever. Do continue."

"That's as far as I've gotten."

Lady Sarah breathed a sigh of relief. Would the Orrs never retire to their own rooms?

"I would like to hear it again," Orr encouraged, "and I know our hero would. It's not everyone who gets his own song, especially one to be sung through the ages. Every line rhymes."

"I shall start from the very beginning, since Lady Sarah and the Reverend will want the full effect."

"Excellent," said the hero.

Lady Sarah bit her lip to keep from groaning, but could not contain a small gurgle of protest. She failed to catch Edward's eye. Once they would have mutually enjoyed such preposterous claims to poetry.

"Ah, Lady Sarah. I knew you would be pleased. Already I feel we are of a mind, bosom-bows, in fact." Aimée Orr paused to prepare for her next assault. "Proclaim the news throughout the land ... " She added gestures to her execution

Lady Sarah retreated to the refuge of the window's relative darkness. She tired of bluffing—a poor defence

at best. Slowly, her serene facade crumbled. Aimée—
doubtless Amy when she was born—Aimée Orr seemed
ageless somehow, the eternal Cyprian. Yet surely she was
no younger than Lady Sarah's eight and twenty years.

Only slightly taller than Lady Sarah's five feet and
three inches, the hussy stood there, vehemently chanting
her dreary tune. Lady Sarah could sing on key. Why,
then, did Edward prefer the one over the other?

It must be the poetry.

Sarah pushed her fingers against her lips to stifle
laughter. The more her serenity faded, the more giddy
she became. Let the record show she could still laugh in
the midst of disaster.

As for the always agreeable Osmond Orr, he hardly
seemed old enough to have fathered clever Amy. If he
carried many years beyond Edward's forty and four, he
carried them well. When had Edward decided he needed
to add this toady to his retinue? A brother and a sister already served admirably in that capacity. Lady Sarah controlled another urge to giggle. In truth, the Smith in-laws
were scarcely a laughing matter.

> To duty always showing devotion,
> He put his battle plan in motion.

Aimée's sweeping gesture, designed to transport one's
imagination to the faraway scene of Edward's monu-
ment-provoking achievement, caught Lady Sarah's
wandering attention. It is neither the blazing diamonds
nor the bright green, she noted, but the woman herself
who glows, actually glows like one who is . . . increasing!
Aimée Orr was with child! Edward's?

With sudden comprehension, Lady Sarah abandoned
all pretence of acceptable social deportment. Through a
blur, she saw the thick waistline in profile and could not
muffle her cry of anguish at the answer to one of tonight's
questions. Aimée Orr was indeed increasing, while Lady
Sarah . . . could not. One must hardly fault Edward for

preferring the mother of his child.

Lady Sarah slumped back against the window curtains, grabbing at the damask drapery for support. It offered none, and she slid to the floor buried in billows of red figured silk. She scrambled to free herself, then stood amidst tittering clucks of concern to confront her husband's eyes, but he refused the engagement.

"My family, Miss Orr, means to draw attention from your heroic saga by whatever means at its disposal. Accept my apologies for the gaucherie, and I pray you continue." Bowing, Bleddem Smith extended his hand, prepared to restore the poetic chronicler to centre stage.

Lady Sarah fought feelings of helplessness, a constant since Edward, trailing his Orrs, had returned to England. She *knew* he had found happiness in their marriage. When had he ceased caring?

"My husband,"Lady Sarah emphasised the words. "My husband, Miss Orr, misunderstands. I am . . . overwhelmed . . . by your rhymes to his heroics. You will excuse me." Further conversation was stilled by the whisper of misty green muslin as she crossed the room to the door, where she paused. "Edward."

Now his eyes met hers, his handsome face unresponsive. Lady Sarah swallowed against a throat suddenly dry. What could she say publicly? Come to me? Gently, she closed the door behind her on the sitting-room, as civilised a wife as society could possibly demand.

How perfect a pairing, Edward. Miss Orr's doggerel celebrating *your* honour!

That is what she should have said.

But she had not. Courtesy was all that remained of their passion. Sarah wept for the loss in the privacy of her chamber.

=2=

THE JUNE BREEZE stirred Lady Sarah's swan's-down muff, wafting another of its white wisps onto Featherstone Smith's serviceable black garb. Having completed purchases at the tobacconist's, they were walking through Mayfair's cheering bustle in the direction of their hotel.

"I vow, Sarah. The happy blush to your cheek exactly matches your pelisse." At her smiling appreciation of his remark, the cleric ventured more. "I imagine you have already forgotten last night's bit of awkwardness." He chuckled. "Your blush matched that fabric, too."

Lady Sarah winced at the memory.

"Now, a rose in rose wool." he crooned.

"A wilted rose, perhaps."

"Never."

No. Never.

Lady Sarah lifted her face to the breeze carrying city smells. After long stays in the country, she liked the contrasts of city life. Nature's immutability healed, while the excitement of the city reminded her that life goes on.

"When shall we see Ned again?" Featherstone Smith queried plaintively.

"I cannot say." When she had gone to Edward's room at first light this morning, nothing indicated he had ever inhabited it, much less slept there.

"Not one exciting battle story has he told us yet."

"But did he not look exactly the hero when they

presented the sword?" Lady Sarah set the old gentleman's mind on a happier track, halting their expedition to stare through the panes of a shop window at confections exhibited there by the town's most sought-after milliner.

"Sarah!" A fashionably dressed matron accosted them, grasping Lady Sarah by the shoulders. "Just what you need, dear friend. A new bonnet. Though I always liked this rose wool turban."

"Toddy! How fine to see you! I meant to call—soon." Lady Sarah reminded her father-in-law, "You know Lady Toddington, our neighbour at Long Wood."

He did not indicate recognition, but stood quietly indulging the friends in their meeting. The accumulation of seventy-six years, added to decades of churchyard cozes after Sunday services, had left him a fairly docile bystander.

"How did you leave your parents?" the elder woman enquired.

"Time has begun its healing, blessedly. I was counting on Edward's coming to make a difference between existing and . . . enjoying." Lady Sarah swallowed and looked away briefly. Her darling brother, killed in the same conflict that brought fame to Edward.

"Edward! Time will help there, too. A passing thing, Sarah."

"Yes," Lady Sarah agreed reluctantly, wondering again about the future of Edward—and of the child *she* was not carrying.

Lady Toddington continued. "We leave for home day after tomorrow. I want you to come with us."

As Lady Sarah shook her head, her friend amended the invitation. "At least let me tell Mrs. Crippen to open up your house. It is where you should be now, away from London, until he realises . . . With your friends to stand by you."

"Toddy, thank you, but I stay with Edward. He and I

have been apart for too long a time."

"And you are together now?" the lady questioned dryly.

Lady Sarah examined more carefully the hats in the window. She would not flee London. Easier to be steadfast of purpose amongst strangers than amidst the sympathy of friends.

"A wife should cleave unto her husband," spoke the man of the church.

Lady Toddington tried another gambit. "You need to be happy, Sarah. You look feverish. Go out and dig again, in the fresh air and sun. Harry says many have guessed that you authored the interesting paper over the signature S.D. Smith, which appeared last year in the Society's *Proceedings*. They look forward to more from you. Think of all the antiquities waiting to be unearthed so you can write more about Ancient Britons. Edward is not the only one deserving of recognition."

She cut short Lady Sarah's demurral. "I hope you have not saved all of Edward's letters for future generations." At Lady Sarah's look of surprise, her friend justified the conversational tack. "Anyone reading his constant complaints over imaginary slights and the politics of advancement might question his heroic stature. You have so competently shielded him from all tedious details of living, Sarah—you nurture his bent for godlike stances."

Her long-standing annoyance satisfactorily diffused, Lady Toddington addressed the obstinate look on Lady Sarah's face with more persuasive tones. "Two days hence. Promise you will think on coming home with us. Father Smith, nice to chat with you. Your son needs a firm hand." She pointed an accusing finger at him before entering the milliner's establishment.

The father, albeit fondly, confirmed Lady Toddington's parting shot. "Sometimes he put me quite out of patience, even when he was in leading strings. *Especially* when he was in leading strings. Whined too much."

Lady Sarah could laugh at the long-suffering parent. Dear Toddy. Had a tendency to tell everyone what to do. If ever Napoleon made good his invasion threat, doubtless she would wait at the shoreline with instructions for him.

Lady Sarah attempted to increase the speed of their stroll, but her father-in-law needed to investigate the buzz of bystanders in front of a print-shop window. Thomas Rowlandson's latest—another representation of an obese Prince of Wales—was centred in the window. To the side, a second caricaturist used Little Bo Peep to ridicule the Bleddem Smith triangle. Searching one side of a haystack was Lady Sarah, looking more like a coronetted Jack Sprat than Little Bo Peep. Coupling out of sight on the other side were a scantily-clad Edward Bleddem Smith with Aimée Orr. A profusion of medals covered Edward's chest. The altered nursery rhyme explained:

> Little Bo Peep has lost her sheep
> And don't know where to find him.
> Will he come home if she leave him alone
> Dragging his tail behind him?
> Barely possible!

"*Barely* possible," one of the viewers snickered.

"He do look to be having himself a fine time," said another, who turned to his stout mate. "Can't blame him, if his wife be that scrawny." A guffaw constituted her reply.

Before an opinion could leave her father-in-law's open mouth, Lady Sarah pulled him away from the offensive display and hurried him along their route towards the hotel. How degrading for Edward—and for her! Was this the reward of fame? Family matters publicly aired? Lady Sarah shook her head. It had become impossible to walk on a public thoroughfare without learning one was universally mocked.

"Sarah! Wait! We go too fast." The gasping divine leaned against his daughter-in-law and regarded her with puzzlement. "I forgot why we hasten," he confessed.

"We hasten to the hotel for a brisk cup of tea."

"Oh. Did we buy Ned's tobacco?"

"Yes. You have it in your pocket."

As they approached their hotel, they were forced to dodge the clattering advance of an open carriage flanked by four outriders. Almost hidden by the horsemen were the Orrs—Aimée, a melange of white and gold—and Edward Bleddem Smith, who waved his hat back and forth above his golden head, inciting one and all to cheer, whether they recognised the war hero or not.

"Ned!" Featherstone Smith doffed his hat to wave at the carriage fast disappearing around the corner. "Did you see him, Sarah? How they cheer! Our Ned." The father's joy lit his face.

Tears of frustration filled Lady Sarah's eyes. Another missed chance to be alone with him. What ever was this Little Bo Peep to do?

She could dig. At Long Wood. Perhaps that would rekindle her interest in the Early Britons. It had been a time-filling and pleasing substitute for motherhood during Edward's long absences chasing war's glory. Had he resented that she dug without him? Long Wood . . . filled with memories of marital bliss. How pleased she had been to find such a good buy for their money when Edward had been on half-pay.

Lady Sarah leaned against the window's frame, watching the dark sky of early morning slowly lighten across a city that long had welcomed her: for her come-out, her wedding trip, during childhood visits to Greataunt Caroline. Now, the welcome had been withdrawn, and Lady Sarah must recognise defeat. Yet, she might still win the war, if only she knew what to do. Of a certain, she would weep no more. It was time, instead, to consider her future.

She must not retire to Devon, where already grieving parents would witness her distress. Even Long Wood held little appeal, filled with Edward's presence and well-meaning friends close by, each with a different version of what was best for her. Nevertheless, she had no other choice. She would leave now, on the first coach headed north. It was pointless to linger in London. Nor did she care to wait for the Toddington's comfortable carriage and long miles of their sympathetic company.

She began to pack, only to stop, suddenly frightened by a ghostly blur. How bird-witted! She had to laugh as she stood before the mirror. Her white robe of sheer wool floated from her shoulders. The room's one pale lamp gave a silver sheen to her unbound hair. *She* was the ghostly blur, the phantom, the non-wife. What had begun in laughter ended as a sob. She stood in the middle of the room, her head bowed. She was not, after all, through with weeping. Would she ever again feel Edward's arms around her?

"Will he come home if she leaves him alone?" she quoted the caricaturist.

"Sarah?"

She looked up to see her father-in-law hesitate in the doorway. She wiped the tears from her face as she straightened her spine. "Father?"

"Are you crying?" Tentatively he crossed the threshold, concern reflected in the round face above his nightshirt.

"Not any more." She sniffled.

"Good." His face brightened. He looked to the bed. "But you are packing?"

"Yes. I leave for Long Wood this morning on the first coach I can obtain. I will send word to Edward that you are alone here, and he will come until G. Featherstone and Emmaline arrive. You remember they are coming, and you will have all your children together again. Grandchildren, too."

"I would rather go with you, Sarah."

She understood his request. He appreciated his children better from a distance, and since his retirement last year in his seventy-fifth year, had preferred to stay with Lady Sarah.

"And not see Emmaline, and G. Featherstone?"

"Yes. Please," he entreated quietly.

In response, Sarah dashed off a letter to her parents, informing them of her return to Long Wood, and a note for Edward detailing the same. She placed it in the middle of his neat bed—the only use there'd been of that piece of furniture since his arrival seven days ago.

===3===

SUSPENDED HALFWAY BETWEEN wakefulness and sleeping, Lady Sarah found respite from further decision making as the swaying coach creaked and groaned its way through a fine mist that soaked the summer countryside. One particularly grating jolt, however, signaled trouble. The vehicle managed to rumble on as far as an inn near the village of Camford, where five grateful passengers descended, only faintly aggrieved at the announced delay in their journey.

Featherstone Smith squinted against the moisture-laden air. "I do not see Ned. Was he to meet us?"

"No, Father. He stayed in London." Oh, to have him here, and the past week nullified! "We go to Long Wood," Lady Sarah prompted as she steered the clergyman after the others into the oblong building of dark stone which bore the sign of The Wise Owl. The Bastille might have looked as forbidding.

She paused by the entrance to glance at the sodden broadside proclaiming an opportunity for cultural enrichment not to be missed. For tonight only, Vauncy Frome, F.R.S., would lecture on the tragedy of England under the Roman yoke. He further promised an authentic depiction of the conquering Julius Caesar. How intriguing. A Fellow of the Royal Society here in this fortress. Perhaps he would welcome a discussion with her during the wait for repair of the coach.

Having settled her father-in-law in front of a large bowl of thick barley soup, from which he contentedly retrieved large chunks of beef, Lady Sarah enquired of the innkeeper the whereabouts of Mr. Frome and was directed to a private parlour.

She opened the door cautiously. "Vauncy Frome?"

Two gentlemen in the wood-panelled room turned from studying a stuffed owl on the mantlepiece above the dying coals of a small fire. Both were conventionally attired, the taller wore a turban framing a face the colour of strongly brewed tea.

"Yes?" answered the shorter of the two. He was a slight man. Curling red hair topped his pale face, frozen for a moment with an apprehension which faded at sight of the slender figure in a rose pelisse, a faint pink tinge to the grey kid gloves on hands clasping her swan's-down muff. Nothing to fear from such elegant femininity, he thought to himself.

Lady Sarah, attributing his fright to a scholar's customary shyness, immediately set to putting him at ease. "I am Mrs. Smith, hoping the vexation of an interruption to my journey north will be allayed by conversation with a Fellow of the Royal Society." She looked past Mr. Frome to his companion, whose sinister mien surely was due only to his unusual visage.

Her introduction further reassured Mr. Frome. Absurd, actually, to have suspected a lady of such obvious breeding to be carrying demands for money. He relaxed and became one who merited initials after his name. "May I present my colleague, Samson? The Great Samson."

"Aptly titled," Lady Sarah smiled her slightly lopsided smile, so at odds with the symmetry of her features, and she walked farther into the room. "I imagine *you* are the authentic depiction of Julius Caesar." Those muscular shoulders and arms should have been draped in a toga rather than encased in the ordinary brown coat he wore.

"I have that task." Bowing, the black man replied in a

low voice, faintly accented.

"And you are from Rome?"

"From within the old Empire," Mr. Frome took over. "We were wondering how to use the owl in tonight's presentation. One must borrow tactics from the stage . . . uh, Mrs. Smith, if one is to successfully capture an audience and then instruct during its captivity."

He walked to one of the windows in the wall opposite the door and looked out on the misty afternoon. "Assuming there is an audience. A lonely mission, Mrs. Smith, spreading knowledge to every corner of the kingdom, and hardly profitable." He sighed, and waited for an expression of sympathetic appreciation, certain it would be forthcoming.

She did not disappoint him. "Lonely, but interesting, surely, Mr. Frome."

He was not as young as he had seemed when seen from a distance. Two deep lines above the bridge of a narrow, pointed nose attested to years of either reading by dim lights or frowning at recalcitrant students.

"Good of you to understand. You entered this dark room, an exquisite rose, blooming to remind us of the beauty in that which is worth doing. *Go, lovely rose,* and tell the world how sweet and fair is learning." He bowed over her hand and escorted her to a Windsor chair near the fire. "An appealing salutation from a seventeenth century poem which comes to mind when you are in view, if you will forgive my familiarity."

Lady Sarah barely inclined her head in acquiescence. "As I said, my father and I wait for repairs required by the coach. It would please us both to hear of your studies."

"But of course, Mrs. Smith." Vauncy Frome's obvious delight completed his transformation from scholar to showman. His eyes sparkled. "Samson, get your chariot to show Mrs. Smith," he ordered. "A remarkable bit of collapsible scenery which he constructed." He called out

to Samson's departing back, "First, order us some . . . "
He turned to Lady Sarah.

On the instant ravenous, Lady Sarah could not remember when last she had wanted food. "Let me bring my father to join us and I will order our refreshments—a replenished fire, as well."

For the next two hours, in The Wise Owl's private parlour, Roman Britain achieved reincarnation at a round table by the fire. Snapping coals punctuated dramatic moments. Vauncy Frome knew his topic, and presented it well.

Samson did not participate in the impromptu seminar but leaned imperturbably against the wall, arms folded over his broad chest. His chariot had won admiration. Painted on a hinged piece of wood three feet square, it had two small wheels attached to the unpainted side, and a small stand on which to rest while Samson assayed his Caesarean depiction. Folded in half, it could be easily transported during their travels.

When the wine bottle next to Vauncy Frome was emptied, that gentleman ended his discourse. Enthusiasm spent, he leaned back in the wooden armchair.

"I have studied the Early Britons of this period," Lady Sarah modestly ventured, not wanting the session to end. Rarely were intellectual encounters possible in her world.

Contented, at last, to yield the centre of attention, Vauncy Frome listened carefully to a short summary of his fellow scholar's digging and conclusions drawn.

"Tell him of the brooch," her father-in-law encouraged with the one thing he could remember from her efforts.

"It was a swan. I had hoped it could be connected to Queen Boadicea, but it has been established as too late for her and most likely is a Plantagenet emblem."

Mr. Frome abruptly sat forward. "I have just had the most unexceptionable notion!" He attempted to refill his glass from the bottle beside him. When nothing poured forth, he turned to his colleague. "See to another bottle, Samson." Samson did not move from the wall.

"Lovely rose. Miss Smith." He conveniently altered her status to fit his fantasy. "I did not know how prophetic I was when earlier this afternoon I bid you tell the world how sweet and fair is learning. You, and your father, must joint us in bringing to our realm its historic heritage. Consider portraying Queen Boadicea to Samson's Julius Caesar," the scholar insisted with an intimacy born of their shared scholarship.

"Caesar was long dead when Queen Boadicea came on the scene," Lady Sarah objected.

The F.R.S. refused to be daunted. "Then Caesar can be—"

"Suetonius Paulinus? He was the Roman governor who defeated Boadicea in the last decisive battle of her revolt."

"Samson can be Suetonius Paulinus. One Roman is as good as another." The *savant* refused to be deterred from planning his spectacle in support of education's advance. "Poisoned herself, as I recall. Oh, I can see it now. You, lovely rose, could die right in front of the audience. A fitting climax to my lecture."

His hands moved to set the scene. "On my right, the Roman governor in his chariot. On the other side emerges our noble queen, with only her sword against the mounted Roman might."

"She and her warriors had chariots also," said Lady Sarah, determined to keep to the facts.

Vauncy Frome, imagination soaring, refused to succumb to accuracy's demands. "Let us drink to . . . to the honourable pursuit of scholarship, and to success therein!" Finding no fresh bottle from which to pour his toast, the scholar-showman querulously beseeched his colleague. "Samson, what happened to the bottle I ordered?"

"Mr. Frome," Lady Sarah rose from her chair. The two

gentlemen courteously followed suit. "We cannot possibly join your . . . endeavour, no matter how honourable the pursuit."

"No, no. Simply would not do." Featherstone Smith placidly supported his daughter-in-law's declaration.

Vauncy Frome ceased rejoicing and wistfully regarded her a long moment. "Oh, lovely rose. Suffer yourself to be desired, and not blush so to be admired." Earnestly, he paraphrased Edmund Waller's poem.

Lady Sarah was uncomfortable with his remarks and his unremitting gaze. Did he know who she was, and her situation? "I must check our departure time." Quickly, she left the room, but the seventeenth-century lines followed her, disrupting her well-ordered mind into a tangle of outlandish thoughts.

Why was it impossible to join his lecture tour, just because it was foreign to everything she had ever done? What would happen if she were to break the conventional pattern of her life? It was easy enough to hide, while changing course, in a name like Mrs. Smith.

But she had no costume for a depiction of Queen Boadicea. And not much money with her, so precipitous had been her departure from London. Yet, wouldn't money be earned—in spite of Mr. Frome's lament?

Suffer *yourself* to be desired and not blush so to be admired. Every thought, every plan in the last decade had as its end the accommodation of Edward. Perhaps it was time to make a decision to suit herself. Let *Edward* wonder where *she* had gone, and whether he would ever see her, hold her again.

Lady Sarah stalked through the fine mist to the stable yard where stage driver, wheelwright, blacksmith, and assorted stable habitués speculated on the likelihood of the coach's continued service. Its need for repair had furnished the high point of the day for many of the quiet hamlet's inhabitants, and the final judgement on its future in transportation was being given parliamentary consideration.

Almost without realising, certainly without thought, Lady Sarah seized the moment and ordered a transfer of the Smiths' baggage to rooms in The Wise Owl, daring anyone to dispute her command. After all, she was not committing herself to a lifetime. There was little to lose if the gambol failed.

The opening move in her rebellion was thus consummated in less time than it took the American colonials at Lexington Green to fire their first shot.

760 4000

═4═

"I CANNOT POSSIBLY retur—go to London." Lady Sarah shook her head to reenforce her refusal.

Intent on persuasion, Vauncy Frome missed her slip of the tongue. "London needs to see how well we recreate the past."

They sat where they could catch the breeze on a small rise overlooking the failing resort town of Madden. When its medicinal waters—hardly bitter enough to seem beneficial—had not drawn crowds, developers turned to the arts with even less success. Certainly there was little welcome from the snarling stone creatures spewing water into a fountain of mediaeval design that fronted a small Greek temple. The latter's classic lines sheltered lecturers who every evening detailed the many paths to ill health. Though scheduling Vauncy Frome represented a departure from the usual fare, the F.R.S. did promise a portrayal of death.

"Oh, Miss Smith. Fame and fortune wait in London. I am certain of it."

"Are fame and fortune our target now? What of your plan to awaken workers in Birmingham and Manchester mills to the pleasures of learning?" Lady Sarah felt better about her decision to have done with the showmanship he piously called scholarship. "Birmingham is so close."

"We cannot ignore the message from our audiences,

Miss Smith. Just think! Attendance has doubled each night since you joined us." The scholar twitched with excitement.

"Since only four people appeared at The Wise Owl, doubling the audience in three subsequent engagements has not proved difficult." Lady Sarah reminded him of reality, a confrontation she herself had been enduring since her impetuous decision at The Wise Owl.

Much of the anger and resentment that had propelled her into this coil was spent now, and she could recognise her precarious situation. How tattlers would rejoice if they knew Lady Sarah Smith cavorted on the very fringes of honest society.

"And a total income of three pounds, four shillings does not even cover expences." Unrelenting, she sought to persuade him of certain truths.

"Three pounds in five days!" Vauncy Frome still gloated. "It took me three months to earn three pounds when I taught . . . once." He said no more, brooding under the sky's high clouds.

"Mr. Frome."

With growing exasperation, Lady Sarah prepared to announce her abdication. Her morning dress of lemon yellow cambric, with raised collar and elbow sleeves, splashed colour against the grassy bank and accented her face, stained Boadicean blue, in the interests of authenticity. She had used a concoction, furnished by the Great Samson, which would not wash off. Her face, as a consequence, grew bluer with the accumulation of performances, and would have excited a whole county's worth of stares had the little troupe not kept to remote inns on back roads in their travels. Lady Sarah amended the tattler's potential gossip—Lady Sarah cavorts blue-faced, on the fringes of honest society!

Yet where was the harm? It was done honourably. In her eyes flashed a strain of Boadicea's defiance against the Romans. Not *all* of Lady Sarah's anger had cooled.

Had there really been thirty-two witnesses to last night's presentation? *Twenty*-two, more likely, thought Lady Sarah. Vauncy Frome knew history, but he could not add—or subtract.

"Tonight," the F.R.S. caressed the word. "Tonight, Miss Smith, there will be sixty-four people come to see us!" He rebounded into optimism, a heedless puppy.

"I doubt there are that many visitors in town. Please, Mr. Frome. Do not expect a large egg from a wren."

The scholar, happily multiplying, did not hear the cautionary adage. "Sixty-four people at three shillings each. That is where I erred, Miss Smith. I should have had faith and never reduced the fee after the calamitous evening at The Wise Owl."

He turned to his cohort. "Perhaps even *more* than sixty-four people tonight!" He scrambled to his feet, stretching out arms to welcome his imaginary horde. "Ladies and gentlemen, do I hear seventy?"

"Mr. Frome."

He ignored her, acknowledging the swell of applause only he could hear.

"Vauncy Frome. Please listen to what I have to say."

He dropped back beside her. "How important my name sounds on your lips."

She smiled her wry grin. How difficult it was to tell him she wanted to leave.

He broke the silence. "I do remember it being your suggestion we use Sunday to reorganise my presentation before continuing on the tour. A wise move—at The Wise Owl." He tittered at his way with words. "And I appreciate your contributions to the new narrative. Really very effective. But you must trust my judgement. I have, after all, been doing this much longer than you, and I say the crowds for your little offering can only increase."

He took hold of her hand that brushed at the grass and held it in both of his. "I am certain after our stay here, I will not have to call on you for any further . . . financial assistance. Rest assured, you will be paid."

"I regard it as costs for my apprenticeship." Lady Sarah removed her hand from his. "It has been an interesting few days, and I have no doubt of your success."

She unfastened the top pearl button at the neck of her dress. It was a muggy day.

"And I think you are right. You *should* go to London, where you can easily find someone to take my place." She drew a deep breath and unfastened a second button. This was hot work. "You can insist on someone more authentic than I, with Boadicea's red hair."

Vauncy Frome stared at her in amazement. "Someone to take your place? Why?"

She could not in kindness declare the many reasons for her growing dislike of their haphazard existence. "Because I find it is not what I want to do. I am not as dedicated to scholarship as you."

"Nonsense. I won't listen to you." He shifted to turn his back to her.

"You know you can find someone who will do more for the depiction of Boadicea." Like Aimée Orr?

"No. No one could appear more regal than you. I simply will not hear of your departure." Refusing to face her, he stood and began walking down towards their lodgings adjacent to Madden's Parthenon.

Relieved, Lady Sarah watched him disappear before giving vent to her grievances. "Zigging and zagging on furrowed back roads at uncomfortable inns take a toll on my patience . . . upon my funds." She stood and brushed at her wrinkled skirts.

"And my poor face. Day by day it turns bluer." All because of her insistence on an authentic depiction of the ancient queen. Well, a pox on customs of the Early Britons!

"A pox on Queen Boadicea—and Edward Bleddem Smith!" She kicked out at the grass. "Oow."

She had forgotten her bruises. There was no easy way

to slump to the floor nightly as a victim of suicide by poisoning. The twinge in her side triggered remembrance of her real husband. She drifted down the slope, engulfed in self-pity, until reason returned and she could withdraw her evil denunciation of Edward. Difficult days, these, yet with little time to dwell on Edward's disloyalty. She thought of him now, with less emotion. War had kept them apart too long to prevent rents in the fabric of their marriage. But could one mend the rips? What was a wife supposed to do while the husband strayed?

Whatever happened, she could face it. Her confidence had revived on the back roads, with Boadicea. Amazing what a little polite applause for the ancient queen could do for Lady Sarah's confidence.

"Father." She approached the old gentleman sitting alone on a bench near the fountain. Obviously, he was enjoying its cool spray.

"Father." Lady Sarah sat down to slip her arm through his. "I have told Mr. Frome we return home. One last night of playing Queen Boadicea and we part company with our learned companions."

The cleric silently contemplated the sparkling droplets. Lady Sarah was content to share the stillness on the esplanade. Moments later she asked, "Are you pleased?"

"Relieved. With all our higgledy-piggledy going about, never staying in the same place more than one night, I feared we might be in dun territory and dodging the bill collectors."

"You didn't!"

"I did. An unsettling time, Sarah. Smiths never renege on their debts."

She sighed. No. Only on their marriage vows.

An hour before the lecture, Lady Sarah applied the damaging ointment to her face and brushed the gloss of brown hair that enveloped her ivory shoulders. She donned the white robe of sheer wool—a makeshift costume, but it did suggest an earlier time—and anchored atop her head the circle of moonstones. Early Britons had worn ornaments of gold, but the shine from the silver filigree acceptably conveyed royalty.

She collected her father-in-law from his supper beside the parlour fire, and the two slipped across to enter an antechambre at the back of the Greek-revival hall. On a narrow wooden bench, between two doors leading to the assembly room, lay a supine Vauncy Frome. One arm and one leg had slipped from the bench to hang above the floor, except where the tips of his fingers and the heel of one black shoe rested. He looked like a dead crow with a rooster's red cockscomb.

"Mr. Frome." Lady Sarah advanced towards her inert colleague. "Mr. Frome." The toe of her slipper nudged a glass bottle, which then rolled farther under Mr. Frome's place of repose.

"*Drink ye, and be drunken, and spew, and fall, and rise no more.*" Featherstone Smith's recall of biblical quotations appropriate for every occasion was remarkable considering the general state of his memory.

At the sound of the latch, Lady Sarah turned to Samson's muscled majesty for deliverance. "Samson. We have a problem."

The Roman general, folded chariot in hand, eyed the comatose scholar. "So I see."

"Will he recover in time?"

Rings on the Roman helmet clanked as Samson shook his head. "He never does."

"We must at least try to—what do you mean 'he never does'? This occurs frequently?" Lady Sarah already knew the answer.

"He should be put to bed," said the vicar.

The helmet clanked once more as Samson nodded agreement. Effortlessly, he carried his charge, only pausing at the door in answer to Lady Sarah's plea.

"You will return immediately?"

He nodded and left. Lady Sarah turned to her father-in-law, but he abstained from any additional quotes. Inching open one of the doors to the assembly room, she peered through the crack. Her prayers—let no one attend—had not been answered. Two separate couples already sat in readiness.

Closing the door, Lady Sarah leaned against it. "Father. It has not been that long since you delivered a sermon. Could you read Mr. Frome's narrative? You have been in the audience each night, and seen how he does it."

She walked to his side and willed him to be truly cognizant of their immediate predicament. "All you have to do is read it."

He frowned. "Is this the Lord's work?"

"No, but He must surely . . . sympathise with our mission!"

"Hummph." He sat down on the bench.

Lady Sarah joined him. "I imagine you could repeat much of it without referring to the manuscript. Ah, Samson. You have Mr. Frome's narration."

"Yes."

"Samson. If you would be both narrator and Roman general, reading from one side of the podium, while I—"

"Oh, mah'm. I can't read."

"Mr. Frome does not teach you?"

He smiled. "I don't think it has occurred to him. I get by fine."

Lady Sarah would have begun plans for his education were it not for the problem closer at hand. "I suggested to Mr. Smith that he might read the narration."

She handed her father-in-law the pages of Mr. Frome's manuscript. "Would you like to read this over?"

"Very well."

The two protagonists expectantly observed the vicar's every reaction to his perusal of the pages. Lady Sarah once more checked the assembly room. Thirteen people had gathered.

"What do you think?" she asked impatiently when the vicar carefully placed the last sheet of paper with the others.

"A good story, Sarah, though a familiar one." He responded to the look of dismay that crossed her face. "I have heard it before, haven't I?"

Oh, dear. She smiled at him. "Yes, you have. Will you read it aloud tonight, the way you used to in church?"

"If you want me to."

When two more head counts were conducted, each indicating fourteen people present, Lady Sarah sought agreement from Samson to begin. The Reverend Mr. Featherstone Smith had not forgotten how to deliver an audible sermon. He faltered, however, at the appearance, each from a separate door, of the armoured Samson rolling his painted chariot board and the white-robed Lady Sarah.

The costumed figures stood silently, facing each other, waiting for the aged cleric to continue, bringing the story into the battlefield. With the one all in white, long hair virginally loose, the Reverend Mr. Smith recognised familiar territory and knew what was called for.

"Dearly beloved, we are gathered together here in the sight of God, and in the face of this company . . . "

Ladies in the audience sighed. How lovely! A wedding, when they were expecting a scold about unhealthful habits.

" . . . to join together this man and this woman in holy matrimony which is an honourable estate . . . "

Lady Sarah, stunned, listened to her father-in-law veer into a marriage ceremony. With great difficulty, she checked her laughter. A glance at Samson showed him unconcerned.

" . . . let him now speak, or else hereafter for ever hold his peace."

Lady Sarah did not speak, but with as much equanimity as she could muster, glided to the lectern and escorted her father-in-law to a seat on the front row, where he settled himself comfortably. She patted his shoulder, then returned to the podium.

Holding tight to the speaker's stand, she looked out at the unperturbed citizens. "General Puesonius—" She paused.

Boadicea would not quake like this. Lady Sarah Davess Smith did not quake like this. She proceeded through the narration, delaying until the very end her death slump. This time, with the lectern to hold to, her fall to the floor was painless but still dramatic. No one in the audience suspected the ad-lib nature of the marriage alliance between the Roman general Suetonius Paulinus and the British queen Boadicea. Nor did anyone question their subsequent clash in battle. History was rife with couples that did not get along. The only harmful aftereffect was to Lady Sarah's complexion, now a shade bluer than earlier in the day. Since her hat box contained nothing designed to hide the exotic condition, she would just have to brazen it out on the public coach tomorrow.

She requested Samson join her in the parlour for a post mortem over late supper. "How long have you played nursemaid to Mr. Frome?" She sought explanations, having abandoned any hope of finding something appetizing on her plate.

"A good long while, mah'm."

"You are not his . . . " She could not bring herself to say the word in this modern world of the nineteenth century. "He does not own you?"

"Oh, no. A law gave me freedom when I arrived here from the West Indies."

"Then why do you stay with him?"

He studied his plate and the remnants of the aged hen that had made the pie so unpalatable. "I see much that I never thought to see. His family, important Bristol merchants, request only that we stay away from there, giving us the rest of the kingdom to roam."

"Merchants in Bristol?"

He nodded. "Generous, to give us all of Britain but Bristol."

Lady Sarah laughed. "Exceedingly. Why you as his companion?"

Samson looked at her from the corner of a wickedly gleaming eye. "Though they were relieved, when I arrived, to see my hair was not red, they thought they detected . . . other family similarities." He boomed laughter at the memory.

Lady Sarah sipped from her glass of weak but cooling lemonade. "I hope you find happiness in this land."

"And you, Mrs. Smith. And you. I think you lack it now."

"Is it so obvious?"

He shook his head. "There is a pinched look to faces of those who . . . are uneasy." He finished his coffee. "You cannot find what you want with us."

"I recognise that." She took another sip of the lemonade. "Has Mr. Frome told you we are leaving?"

"When?" He leaned forwards.

"In the morning. Tonight was my farewell performance."

The Great Samson arose from the table and bowed. "Good. A safe journey, Mrs. Smith."

Lady Sarah remained in her chair after he had left and reviewed the morrow's plans. They must travel northwest until they made the connexion for Ludbury. She would be uneasy until they were again heading north and east towards Long Wood.

=5=

"THE RECKONING, MR. Harderbeck, please. Mr. Smith would like to settle our account." Lady Sarah customarily promoted the fiction that he handled their finances.

"Ah, yes. Here y' are. Mr. Frome said you'd see to it."

"He has come down, then." Lady Sarah glanced about, wanting an amicable parting with Bristol's black sheep.

"Why, he left, 'bout two hours ago."

"What?"

"Mr. Frome left with that Arab 'bout two hours ago. They said 'twas urgent."

All traces of geniality disappeared from Harderbeck's long face. Bushy brows met at the furrow above his nose. "You didn't know?"

One finger followed the square neckline of her blue printed cotton dress as Lady Sarah tried to shake off a sense of impending disaster. First Edward's desertion, now this.

"Payments are made here in real money, Mrs. Smith. No fancy bits of paper not worth your brass farthing." She seemed like gentry, but Harderbeck would not be taken in by those clear grey eyes. Her blue face marked her as theatrical, and that kind were trickier than gypsies.

Despite careful application of arithmetic, the bill still amounted to more money than remained in Lady Sarah's purse. "I presume the hire of a horse and gig listed here was for Mr. Frome's urgent matter."

The host nodded. "Real money, Mrs. Smith."

She smiled at the dun-coloured length of him. "I shall apprise Mr. Smith."

If only it were possible, to apprise him and have him come to the rescue. And if wishes were horses . . . then they could just ride out from here.

Numerous responses, all of them foolish, chased through Lady Sarah's mind as she mounted the stairs to their rooms. Never talk rich, never talk poor, never talk money. Those were her mama's words, and an appropriate conceit for her papa's pocket earldom. I regret, Mr. Harderbeck, but I never talk money. I merely bloom like a lovely rose.

Having reached the corridor, she encountered a gentleman of rather short stature exiting his room. He halted at the sight of her. Surely a blue face was not that uncommon. Lady Sarah swept past him.

"Lady—Mrs. Smith?" he sputtered.

Lady Sarah's heart stopped, or seemed to. She almost wished it had. Edward would never forgive her if word of this indecorum gained wide enough circulation to delay promotion. She should have pretended deafness and continued on to her room but instead, thoughtlessly turned to gaze with courteous tolerance at a prettily handsome face above an exquisite cravat and well-cut coat of bottle green. He looked just the sort of dandy to relish being first with the latest *on dit*.

"Did you address me, sir?"

"Lady Sarah Smith, is it not?"

"You mistake me." Wheeling, she slipped through the door into her father-in-law's chambre hoping the beau could never be certain of her identity, given the corridor's poor light and the brevity of their encounter.

It was the elegant Lady Sarah and no mistake. He had attended a reception some years ago where that gracious courtesy put every junior officer at ease. Charles Trimmer fidgeted with the square-cut onyx centred in the intricate folds of his neck-cloth and continued down to the ground floor. What did Bleddem Smith's aristocrat wife do here and with a blue face? Incognito, or was it all the crack to match face colour to dress? He had been gone from London too long to know.

"Harderbeck!" he barked at the innkeeper hovering near the foot of the stairs. "I am almost certain your cook is the same rogue who continually tried to poison me while I fought the French. Urge him to fix me a breakfast that does not bring on life-threatening illness, or I will have his hide and yours."

Trimmer pushed through the door of the establishment's sparsely furnished private parlour and proceeded to wander its perimeter until Harderbeck, of a colour with dust, entered carrying a breakfast order of the same hue. The beau sneered as he regarded the plate and shrugged before he sat at a table near windows overlooking the side terrace.

"I am too good-natured, Harderbeck."

The host stood by, ready to fend off complaints while Trimmer's fork poked among the plate's various mounds.

He retrieved a piece of ham from the grey sauce and enquired casually, "Has Mrs. Smith been down to break her fast this morning?"

"Maybe she can't."

"Oh? Hasn't the stomach for it?"

"Maybe she can't 'ford it."

"Can't afford it? Why?"

"Left in the lurch, maybe. Turned a bit green when she was left with the reckoning."

Enos Harderbeck did what he could to foster sound financial practices and titillating rumours for those giving Madden their custom. It was not his fault the spa failed to achieve the popularity of a Bath or Cheltenham.

"Hm," said Trimmer.

Confirmation. And was the Lady Sarah giving tit for tat to the self-satisfied snow bank she called husband? Which turned out poorly, did it? She needed lessons in how to choose a good man. Trimmer brushed back the sides of his onyx-coloured hair, cut in the Brutus style. She needed more experience. He reflected on this, taking a sip of coffee.

"Harderbeck! No one who values sound health can afford your fare. This coffee tastes like pea soup. Bring me ale. I doubt you have any decent wine."

The host scurried to comply. Trimmer applied his napkin to a mouth most appealingly curved before he relaxed against the back of the armchair. Somewhere in Lady Sarah's predicament lay profit for him. What would the oh-so-proper hero pay to learn of his wife's dalliance? It would be easy enough to create a scandal. A few well-phrased whispers in a few well-chosen ears, and who would know false from true?

Trimmer returned to the onerous task of selecting another morsel from his breakfast plate. Oh, the drawbacks to travel in the provinces!

On the other hand, he must take care that nothing he did would benefit Bled 'Em Ned Smith.

=== 6 ===

"I BELIEVE I am seeing the queen of the gods," Featherstone Smith informed his daughter-in-law, who had just entered his chambre and leaned against its closed door, her hands pressed against a face unusually pale. "I believe *you* have seen a ghost."

She shook her head and joined him by the window, where he sat watching below while two men wrestled with a tufted couch of light blue so grandly sized it could not be manoeuvred through the rear door of Madden's temple of learning. Nor did the wide-brimmed hat atop a tall female allow for graceful passage through the door. The Juno, all in white except for red spots the size of shillings on her monstrous hat, promptly solved the dilemma, leading the two men and their immense ottoman towards the front of the miniature Parthenon where wide double doors ensured successful entry.

"A clever queen, too, demonstrating the direct route is the best route." Lady Sarah's unquiet heart found comfort in the happy conclusion to the quandary below.

There was really no cause to worry over such a minor incident. The dandy in the hall had probably forgotten her already. Why must she constantly fear Edward's reaction, as if he had kept her in thrall all these years?

"I know we travel today." Her father-in-law indicated their baggage by the door. "Do we wait for Ned?"

"No. We wait for me to marshal my forces."

There was the moonstone necklace which she could leave as surety against their debt. It was her only solid link to Edward's love for her, but a debt-free departure took precedence over sentiment. She retrieved from her trunk the small leather case, inlaid with tortoise shell, which held the last of their travel money, and the moonstones.

Gripping the gold-stamped leather handles, she marched back down the stairs, prepared to inform Mr. Harderbeck of her means for settling the bill. Then, a safe retreat to Long Wood, and she could mark paid to a week of imprudence—a strange week, which had brought her a measure of certainty she had been lacking.

She was still unsure of her future, but not so disheartened. She would manage. And, if a sullied reputation was to be her lot, she wondered whether she would care, even for Edward's sake. Enhancing his reputation, he would remind her, was her responsibility. Not for *his* wife the dampened petticoats that so revealingly clung. Well, let *him* deal with his reputation!

"Mr. Harderbeck."

This was going to be difficult. The innkeeper's intractable face seemed carved from granite. Or was it just the darkness of his lair under the stairs?

Lady Sarah gripped the high counter which separated them. "Mr. Harderbeck. I would like a word with you," she came close to squeaking the demand.

"You'll have it, Mrs. Smith."

She straightened her shoulders. "Good. Mr. Harderbeck. As you no doubt have guessed, I find myself temporarily without the funds to meet expences incurred here." How very businesslike she sounded, how in command. "But I have this silver necklace of moonstones . . . "

She lifted the piece from the stiff leather case and lay it lovingly on the black wood of the counter where the stones gleamed elegantly. It would not do to remember the day when they were presented to her.

"I have every intention of redeeming this, for it was . . . I value it. More than . . . I value it highly. It should more than cover what is owed you."

Harderbeck looked at her earnest face and clear grey eyes, and then at the shining jewels. He pulled out a piece of paper upon which he wrote with a considerable flourish.

"These are the terms of redemption. You have thirty days 'fore I take it as my own."

He studied her flushed cheeks while she folded the paper and placed it in the leather case.

"You may need this." From his waistcoat pocket he handed her a guinea. "In case you're 'thout funds thirty days from now."

"Mr. Harderbeck, this is not necess—"

"Not 'nother word. I' preciate beauty as much as the next 'n."

"Mr. Harderbeck. You are misnamed," Lady Sarah acceded. Her smile was, as usual, out of proportion with the delicate beauty of her features. "You *will* take special care of the necklace while it is in your hands?"

All geniality had returned to the long stretch of Harderbeck's face. He nodded, but could not resist the opportunity for moral instruction. "If your father had sense—which o' course, he hasn't—he'd take you home. Or do you have a home? Is that how the pair o' you come to wander where you don't b'long?"

"We have a home, to which we go on the midday coach."

"See that you do."

"And you will be surprised, Mr. Harderbeck, at my prompt redemption of the necklace."

"Humph." He gave his attention to locking it in a large metal box.

Well! That had not been so difficult after all, and the innkeeper proved surprisingly kind. Lady Sarah's sense of accomplishment ran wild until she reached the top of the stairs.

"Ooooo!"

The queen of the gods, less regal than she appeared from the widow, went into a trance at sight of Lady Sarah.

"I beg your pardon." Lady Sarah tried to slip around the six feet of young womanhood topped by three feet of hat brim.

"Oh, yes." The huge spotted hat vibrated briefly, until Juno came back to life. "How perfect!"

"Perfect?"

"Your face. How long has it been blue?"

The recent chain of disasters had overset Lady Sarah's inclination to ignore such blandishment. "Too long," she admitted.

"It calls everyone's attention to you." The younger woman hastened to point out this advantage.

"I know."

Lady Sarah laughed ruefully and began to walk towards the door to her bedchambre. Her admirer walked along with her.

"Was it your idea—to have a blue face?"

"No. It was Queen Boadicea's."

"Queen who?"

"Queen Boadicea. She was a ruler in this land more than a thousand years ago." Lady Sarah opened the door.

"Fancy that! I lived in Italy once, in another life, maybe a thousand years ago. I can't be sure."

Astonished, Lady Sarah had to enquire. "How do you know?"

"One of Charles' clients told me. From Italy he was. Said I was like that volcano there, and called me Vesuvia 'cause I set him on fire." Having followed Lady Sarah into the room, the former volcano scanned the surroundings. "I like the name. Gives me dis—dis—. Makes me memorable. Don't you agree?" the artless young creature asked.

"Yes. Who is Charles?"

"I work for him in The Celestial Bed."

Understanding evolved. Is she, could she be . . . .?

"I think I have seen it. How old are you, Vesuvia?"

"Seventeen or eighteen, I believe." Her eyes lit on the lone jar sitting on a small table. She opened it. "Is this what made your face blue?"

"Yes." Lady Sarah had planned on leaving it to be discarded. "Would you like it?"

"Oh, yes! How much shall I pay you for it?"

"It is yours. I give it to you."

Vesuvia clutched the jar of ointment to her breast. "How good of you!"

"If I were truly good, I would try to persuade you to find some other line of work."

"Oh, I don't plan to stay with Charles too long."

"I am so pleased to hear that."

"I want to go where it's warm. Naples. That's where Signor Dusty, Charles's client, said I should be. I'm saving to go."

Lady Sarah thrust out the hand in which Harderbeck's guinea still rested. "Perhaps this will help you leave Charles even sooner. Would your Italian friend help you find honourable work?"

"Honourable?" Puzzlement flitted across that part of Vesuvia's face not hidden by her hat. "I worked for a milliner before Charles, but she was not honourable. Mean to me, she was."

"A milliner."

"Yes. I made this hat. What do you think?" Vesuvia lowered her head to allow Lady Sarah a better view. "It's my masterpiece."

Lady Sarah swallowed. "Most unique."

"Unique. Yes. I've never seen one with a wider brim."

"Nor have I." Lady Sarah expressed her complete agreement.

From the open window, the throb of traffic signified a

steady trickle of arrivals come to test The Celestial Bed's vaunted healing powers, and Vesuvia responded. "I'd like to stay, but Charles must see how I look with a blue face."

She stopped at the door. "How nice you've been to me. I wish we could be friends. But Charles and I, we travel too much." Wistfully, she confessed to the loneliness of the road.

"We did have a few friendly minutes together," Lady Sarah consoled.

"That's true. But I don't even know your name."

"Sa—Mary."

"Good-bye, then, Samary. I hope I look as good as you with a blue face. And thank you for the guinea." She held it up before she shot through the door.

Oh, that the cheery thing would keep to her determination to leave her present occupation! Lady Sarah felt greatly encouraged by a world which held such amicable interludes. She had been similarly determined at eighteen—determined to marry Edward, who had charged into her life straight out of some fairy tale and then sailed off to the Indies, Egypt, lands as strange and distant as those in the stories.

"I wish I had been less determined," Lady Sarah voiced her thoughts and hoped she and her father-in-law would not need emergency funds between here and Long Wood, though she did not regret the gift of the guinea. "I dreamed too much, when I was eighteen."

The midday coach would return her to the realities of being twenty-eight and without her husband's regard.

=7=

JACK RUTLAND MOVED out from the dark taproom into the early morning sunshine on a small terrace above the stream bordering Madden. He stood, one booted foot on the low stone ledge, and watched the water's incessant flow, as inevitable as triumph. He savoured the word.

Another day for turning up trump. Little more than three years since he had won Gaunt's estate in a card game. Fitting that the last of Gaunt's mortgage could be paid off with proceeds from the sale of his cellar. Madden's determined developers now sought, by means of fine wine, to gain renown for their spa.

Rutland stretched his arms. Broad shoulders strained against the worn fabric of his blue broadcloth coat. A long ride ahead and more to master tomorrow—and tomorrow, and tomorrow. It was not yet time to celebrate. No matter. He had rescued eight hundred neglected acres, restoring landed status to the disinherited line from which he descended. That was what mattered.

He inhaled deeply of the fresh air. After a night of negotiations in suffocating tobacco smoke, he needed the cool tang as tonic.

"Rutland?"

He turned towards the intruding voice.

"Jack Rutland. by all that's holy!" Smiling broadly, Charles Trimmer emerged from the private parlour.

The Helder campaign . . . in Holland. Rutland had encountered the fellow during the bungled army-navy expedition with the Russians, but could not recall his name. "A fine one you are to talk about holy," he parried, a certain harshness in his speech.

Charles Trimmer laughed appreciatively. Pleasure at what he perceived as an immediate resumption of officers' camaraderie spread across his handsome face. "Oh, yes. Those card games would make a parson blink. Still the wild man at the gaming table?"

"No. The parson smiles when he sees me now." Rutland further recalled that one protected one's rear against this dandy, but the name eluded him.

"Hardly the Jack Rutland I remember. I hope you will let me recoup some of my losses."

"Losses? Were you not the one winning enough to buy Russia? I thought you would be Tsar by now."

"Gammon! Why not one deal of the cards for old times' sake?"

Rutland shook his head. He had not played since winning Gaunt's land. "No challenge for you in a game with me. I have forgotten how many cards to the deck."

Charles Trimmer looked up at the sun-streaked brown hair. My God, did he labour in the fields? The simply tied neck-cloth, the less than fashionable cut to the coat on the man whose rugged nonchalance had incited envy. It was a pity, really, to find such derring-do fallen on hard times and proved the fallacy of following honour's path.

"I presume you no longer serve in His Majesty's forces."

Rutland nodded. "When peace seemed possible, I turned to other concerns." And a haphazard life it had been, but at least he ended a career dependent on the posturing of kings and corporals.

"Ah, yes. The peace." The curvaceous lips formed a sneer. "I frequently toast the Treaty of Amiens. During that lull in our quarrel with the French revolutionists, I, too, became my own master."

"I would ask for details of your obvious success were it not for the long ride ahead of me." Jack Rutland edged closer to the taproom's double doors. "Remarkable to see you here and thriving."

"You would not hurry your departure if you knew my current interest."

The dandy's face reflected a supreme confidence Rutland had not seen since the fiasco in Holland. "If you were parading Napoleon at the end of a rope, I still could not tarry," he confessed with a laugh.

"Let me mention six feet of the most magnificent curves you have ever seen, appropriately named Vesuvia. Claims to have emerged from volcanic ash . . . in another life."

"Never say you export Haymarket-ware to the provinces. Believe me, we have our own high-fliers."

Trimmer. Rutland remembered. The name was Charles Trimmer. An opportunist, surely, but even he would not sink to such a rig.

"I am in therapeutics," Charles Trimmer protested, "with the Celestial Bed. Though I sincerely doubt you have any great need of my remedies, you should see what brings in thirty pounds per private session."

"I have heard of its wonders."

Thirty pounds! Finances held the high ground in Jack Rutland's thoughts. He had begun to long for some of the amenities of life that money could buy, like a house. The hapless Lord Gaunt had put his mansion to the torch, leaving only smoking vestiges of a once noble seat to welcome Rutland. He could still remember the sting in his nostrils, the wrenching disappointment in his gut. Thirty pounds and he could lease additional acres or hire a builder with a pattern book . . . a cook.

Rutland shook off the daydream, a characteristic smile of self-mockery marking his return to the day's practicalities. He was grateful for his solid investment in eight hundred acres.

"The only bed tempting me this day is the one at the end of my ride." It would be mid-afternoon, as it was, before he reached his Chance with enough reserve strength to see him through the last of the post-sheep-shearing celebrations. "I guess I grow old before my time, Trimmer. A decrepit shell of the man you once encountered." He eased nearer the target doors.

"Decrepit!"

Trimmer threw his head back and laughed. Though he had never met a man he liked, he came close to admiring this man's relaxed humour, even in the worst of times. And there had been grim days on the Helder.

"Charles! What do you think?" A statuesque young Venus in white muslin charged onto the terrace, curving arms lifted outwards.

"What do I think of what?" he responded, eyes assessing her body.

"My blue face! Don't you think it makes me look more celestial?" Now she turned languorously, peering over her shoulder under short dark curls that bobbed in support of her enthusiasm.

Trimmer shrugged. Eyes still fixed on the play of sunlight over her undulating form, he called out to Jack Rutland. "Did I exaggerate in describing Vesuvia?"

"No, indeed," rasped Rutland, clearing a suddenly restricted throat. He was not as decrepit as he claimed. Amusement sparked his dark blue eyes and coaxed the corners of his mouth back into its wry smile. Her body held promise of sure cures for any number of man's infirmities, but thirty pounds? He wondered at the advantage of bedding a woman with a blue face.

"A friend *gave* me a jar of it. Said she didn't need it any more." Vesuvia gloried in her bargain.

A friend? thought Charles Trimmer. Lady Sarah? Or were blue faces, indeed, the newest fashion? He must try it, then.

"Wasn't that lucky for me?"

Abandoning hope of praise from Trimmer, Vesuvia turned her attention to the stranger present. She circled him, keeping her back to him while glancing coyly over her shoulder. The blue face accentuated the whites of dark eyes feigning adoration, like a clown, having fun with the art of seduction.

Jack Rutland found it difficult not to laugh at her. Was it the bright sunshine that took away the mystery? If Trimmer did not aim for satire, he should shift his eyes to this *naif*'s face. She could win a laugh from one of Cromwell's Puritans.

"Vesuvia, this is Mr. Rutland. He and I were once enmeshed in the same campaign against Napoleon."

"Are you a client for The Celestial Bed?" Vesuvia continued to circle her prey.

"Lord, no!" The vehemence of Rutland's outburst covered some of his laughter. He longed for deliverance as she persisted in the attempt to tantalise under Trimmer's benevolent gaze.

Enough! Rutland's long fingers grabbed her upper arms, pulling the back of her against the front of him. He kissed the nearest earlobe then shoved her forwards, releasing her.

"You would be too much for me, Vesuvia. Even after a treatment in your Celestial Bed." He grinned at the promoter. "You are not enmeshing me in this campaign, Trimmer."

Rutland strode from the sunlit terrace and was still chuckling when he reached the stable. There were times—coming more often lately—when he wished a wife awaited him at Chance. Not just any wife, but a special one, liking what he liked—children, and building a dream. In a year or two, when a house was ready, he would go looking for her.

Lady Sarah shielded her eyes against the bright sky as the sound of the coachman's horn warned of its imminent arrival.

To be free of Madden at last! Thank heaven no one had recognised her during the sojourn here. Would Vesuvia connect her friend Samary with one Lady Sarah Smith? Samary, a model of propriety? Lady Sarah swallowed her delight behind gloved fingers.

In the rose wool pelisse she more nearly resembled a lady in the first stare of fashion, except, of course, for the dyed-blue face. Her small turban of the same soft rose wool pelisse concealed neither her face nor much of the lustrous, brown hair pulled into a thick coil at the nape of her neck.

"I suppose Ned is still busy and cannot accompany us on our travels." Featherstone Smith's smiling face clouded. "You should speak to him, Sarah."

"I wish I could."

What would she say? Edward, we slink out of town because I have been exceptionally foolhardy and brought disgrace upon us. Just as well he was not here.

"If you do not, I will." The cleric's mild threat dissolved in the sunlight, replaced by the welcome sound of the approaching coach, the slap of reins, the snorting of horses.

Soon, Lady Sarah's uneasiness could diminish.

"And where do we go today?" the Reverend Mr. Smith repeated his morning *ave*.

"To Ludbury."

They must continue in a northwesterly direction towards Manchester, until connecting with a coach going north and east to Ludbury.

"Ludbury?"

"Where we spend the night. Tomorrow we reach Long Wood, and end our travels." Lady Sarah hugged her father-in-law around the shoulders. "You can drop anchor in the sun parlour forever, if you wish."

"I rather enjoyed our stay here. Pleasant prospects everywhere."

Perhaps, thought Lady Sarah, assisting him into the

coach, but pleasant prospects were easy to find. Long Wood had many. Nonetheless, prospects of a safe port did not gladden Lady Sarah's heart in spite of her relief at departing Madden and the lecture circuit. She wanted to sail off, with a husband, experiencing love again, and tenderness . . . and passion. Damn Edward! She wanted to feel happy and at one with . . . with someone. Where was that in her future? She shook her head. It was too daunting to think of the future.

"Samary! Oh, Samary!"

A blue-faced Vesuvia, carrying her outlandish spotted hat, scuttled any plans of leaving quietly. Lady Sarah removed her foot from the coach step and drew on a dwindling reserve of *noblesse oblige* to smile in response.

"Vesuvia."

"I was afraid I had missed you! Here!" She shoved the hat at Lady Sarah. "I want you to have it. Like we were friends trading gifts."

"Oh, no, Vesuvia. Your masterpiece. You will need it in Italy."

Black curls bounced as the designer shook her head. "Please take it, and remember me." Black eyes suddenly lost their animation. "You said you liked it. Unique, you said."

"Oh, Vesuvia. I do like it, and thank you. And no one could ever forget you."

As the two embraced, Lady Sarah fought back tears, not only for the younger woman's sacrifice of her hat, but also at having to transport the unwieldy reminder of a futile rebellion.

"You get settled inside, and I'll hand it to you through the door." Vesuvia's volcanic spirit had returned, and the manoevre was successfully accomplished.

"Put it on. Let me see how it looks."

The Gargantuan brim hit against the Reverend Mr. Smith's headgear, knocking it askew, and blocked the view of a sober-faced countryman who dodged to keep his eyes on the hamper in his lap. From the coach's interior issued a series of clucks as the coach began to roll.

"Good-bye, Samary!" Vesuvia's cheerful cry faded as the coach gained speed. "Saa-maary. Good-byy-y-y."

Lady Sarah removed the gift hat to hold it upright in front of her, preventing any view of the seat opposite. This was almost like having a private carriage, she thought, and wished the coach would take them directly to Long Wood's front entrance. She would not draw an easy breath until they were travelling in a northeasterly direction on the main road. She resolved to again remind the coachman at the next stop to let them off at the Ludbury crossroad.

Still, he forgot, and the coach had barrelled along in the opalescent twilight for some few minutes before the combined efforts of the inside passengers gained his attention. The Smiths and their belongings were dropped off with the grudging advice that the walk back was not that far.

Not far? And how were they to transport their baggage?

=8=

"NED IS LATE in meeting us." Featherstone Smith perched uncomfortably atop his worn valise by the side of the road and watched as Lady Sarah stood contemplating the small trunk, her hat box, and dressing bag. With that huge hat on her head, the fact that her face was stained blue should escape notice, he decided. Not the kind of thing Sarah usually wore, but it did hide the blue face.

"Was Ned to be here?" he asked again.

"No, Father. He is still in London. We travel home to Long Wood." She jogged his memory.

"Oh. Yes." So much easier to remember the long ago. He scanned the quiet summer landscape. From both sides of the deserted road, fields sloped gradually up to woods beyond. "How will we get there?" he enquired matter-of-factly, demonstrating an unswerving confidence in his daughter-in-law's ability to see to things.

"I am thinking on it," Lady Sarah replied as calmly as she could. They would have to abandon what they could not carry—a fit end to her brief rebellion against . . . what? Common sense?

The sound of approaching voices reached them moments before two stocky figures appeared ahead where the road curved. Lady Sarah looked expectantly in their direction and prayed they would be honest and willing to help. The pair halted at first sight of such unexpected flotsam on the isolated road and began to confer. Their unwillingness to proceed, coupled with apparent plotting, chilled her. She shivered, the pelisse of rose wool suddenly inadequate in the balmy evening air, and moved closer to the frail but male presence of her father-in-law. Perhaps it was the hat. Cautious rustics would not know what to make of it. She took it off, remembering too late the blue-stained face which the broad brim had hidden.

"Sarah, someone comes to meet us after all!"

The longtime servant of God arose from his seat, ready to greet the approaching men. Having ended their conference, they strode down the road. One marched just to the side and a step behind the other.

"I devoutly hope so, Father."

Without horses, the two men could hardly be highwaymen. Lady Sarah took comfort in this. From about fifteen feet away, the duo paused again to study the Smiths and their baggage. Clothed decently enough, both strangers were in knee breeches. The one in the forefront, in jacket and oversized tricorn hat, dominated the other, in the smock of a country labourer.

Relinquishing her hold on the huge, spotted hat, Lady Sarah picked up the only weapon in sight, the valise. Shaking hands grasped the handle as she held the case in front of her.

"Well met, my good men," said the country vicar, who over the years had welcomed many a parishioner to church. He walked forwards in greeting.

"We will be grateful for your assistance," Lady Sarah called out. She took a deep breath to quiet her racing heart. "We need to return to the crossroads to catch a coach for Ludbury."

"A likely tale," said the leader, who stalked past Featherstone Smith's outstretched hand to confront Lady Sarah, "but not likely to fool Derby W. Stout, Deputy Constable."

"I assure you—"

"Boney's spies scurrying all over this land, trying to invade us, and you're wanting me to believe you're out here *with your face blackened* waiting for a coach ride!" He interrupted. "It's a capital offence to be out after dark with your face blackened."

He tucked in his chin to observe the effect his bombast had on the odd-looking female. If she wasn't in disguise, he didn't know disguise, and he did.

"But my face is *blue,* not black!" Lady Sarah replied astonished, but a trifle more at ease knowing he represented local government rather than criminal elements in the area.

"See here, good fellow," Featherstone Smith spoke placatingly, "I believe you have drawn conclusions too hurriedly. We are not spies." He chuckled kindly. "Far from it. We—"

The deputy constable turned on the clergyman. "Where's your church located, parson?"

"Why, I am—I no longer—I ret—" the Reverend Mr. Smith sputtered, never before having been denied the honour accorded his sober black garments, his collar.

"Aha!" Deputy Constable Stout pounced triumphantly. "You think I don't recognise disguises when I see them? If ever I saw two people out of place, it's you two!" His vehemence fed on itself. Visions of a shiny medal on his coat for all to see, danced in his head.

"Exactly, Deputy Constable," Lady Sarah agreed in her most dulcet tones. "We admit to being out of place. We find ourselves in this uncomfortable situation because of a forgetful coachman. Did a coach not pass you on the road ahead? It was to have left us at the Ludbury crossroads—" She halted her reasonable explanation at the upraised hand of the deputy constable, who held his palm as if he would dam the torrent of her words while his cohort whispered in his ear.

"Good thinking." Derby W. Stout nodded at his assistant before again addressing the stained face of his passport to the nation's undying gratitude. Napoleon Bonaparte's evil agents could not bamboozle Deputy Constable Derby W. Stout. "Holding onto that valise mighty carefully. What's in it?"

Lady Sarah immediately dropped the questioned item and stepped back. "Please inspect its contents."

Assuming Napoleon's agents had no need of clean unmentionables, nothing of incriminating interest resulted from the careful search. A halfhearted examination of the rest of the baggage followed. The deputy constable dismissed dreams of his carved likeness reclining atop a stone coffin in the parish church.

Lady Sarah sensed his disappointment. As vindication and relief surged within her, she considered repeating her request for aid in reaching Ludbury. Doubtless they had by now missed the coach at the crossroads.

"Sarah," her father-in-law sighed wearily, "I do not think Ned is coming. I would like to retire." The sight of his nightshirt in the open valise had proved impossible to resist. "Could we find an inn and complete our journey tomorrow?"

"Ned? Who's Ned?" the deputy constable demanded. Dying embers of his dream reignited.

"His son," Lady Sarah replied resignedly. "Please. My father-in-law suffers from the confusion of the very old. Help us to an inn where he can rest, and we will resolve this *contretemps*."

"There's no overlooking your black face," said the deputy constable, in retaliation for her use of the fancy foreign word he did not quite understand. "A capital offence."

"It is *not* black. It is blue. And it is not yet dark."

Would this never end, this foolish scene from some Shakespearean comedy? She was hot, yet she shivered. When had she last eaten? How funny. She could not recall. Getting as bad as her father-in-law. Unquestionably, she felt light-headed. She had to sit down for a minute. Lady Sarah plopped down on the small trunk. Let these minions of the law do whatever was necessary to carry out their duty. She would sit first.

This proved as effective a tactic as some for which Edward Bleddem Smith was being fêted in London. Unsure of their next move, the deputy constable and his aide stared in silence at the lady drooping on the trunk. During the ensuing silence, Featherstone Smith closed his valise after first removing his nightshirt to drape over an arm.

Deputy Constable Stout deliberated. For certain her face was blue. Would a spy have a blue face? Maybe the pair of them were not right in the head. He had recognised the delicate fabric and fine stitching of her—Stout cleared his throat against a momentary constriction—thing, in the trunk. They were gentry all right, and gentry could be very odd, very eccentric.

"Ay, he'll know what to do," he concluded. "We'll ask Jack Rutland." Stout looked up at the woods. "This is his land, and he'll know what to do. Probably used to dealing with spies. And always has something for a parched throat."

The murmur of Derby W. Stout's whispered remarks to his assistant accompanied the odd caravan that trudged west around the curve in the road, then north along the incline of a tree-lined drive, rutted from neglect. The two men led the way, carrying between them the small trunk. The aide had the valise and the dressing bag. Lady Sarah, believing the tide might have turned in her favour when the men had condescended to bring the baggage, bore the burden of the wide-brimmed hat on her head and the hat box on her arm. Featherstone Smith, nightshirt at the ready, kept pace by her side.

Unless this Jack Rutland was as close-minded as the idiots ahead, as a landowner he would recognise the Smiths for the quality they were and assist them on their way. Nevertheless, Lady Sarah wondered if morning would find them still alive, and in irons. She had little occasion to be familiar with the nation's system of justice, except when Edward would refer to the swift punishment given deserters.

"Be dark soon,"the Reverend Mr. Smith commented. "I hope the inn is not far."

"Yes." Lady Sarah had no strength to say more. The hat, the ridiculous hat, grew heavier on her head. Hard to keep her balance. She stumbled in a rut and staggered against her father-in-law. His hands, surprisingly firm, steadied her.

"How can they expect our custom if they do not maintain their drive," he fretted over the neglected track.

They passed between stone pedestals that once must have anchored a gate. Erosion had obliterated the carved stone crests, but remnants of a charcoal scrawl on one spelled CHANCE.

Onwards, and ahead to the right, fluted columns in support of nothing stood tall against a last vestige of the twilight's pearl-hued sky. Back of the columned portico, smoke-blackened walls testified to a fire's destruction.

"No sign of life nor light. Cheese-paring economies," said Featherstone Smith, disturbed. "I do not think this place will please us, Sarah."

Lady Sarah could think of no reply. To what kind of landowner was she planning an appeal for aid? She had been able to cope with all the buffetings of the past days, but her growing apprehension was another matter altogether. How did she cope with cold fear? She rested her hand on her father-in-law's shoulder. Its warmth lessened her panic. She could scarcely see his face as he turned in response to her gesture.

"Thou shalt not be afraid for the terror by night," he answered her touch.

A bend in the drive brought the pilgrims to the side— or was it the back?—of the ruined mansion where double doors of wood opened wide to the evening air, permeated with the scent of lilacs. The sweet fragrance helped allay Lady Sarah's fear. Would lilacs flourish where there was evil?

The deputy constable and his assistant dropped the Smiths' baggage, and Stout removed his tricorn hat as he rapped loudly on one of the double doors. "Ho! Mr. Rutland!"

There was a rasp in the voice that answered back. The law's minions escorted the Smiths across a stone-flagged porch into a large ballroom, its former glory still apparent by the light from a candle-laden silver candelabrum on the long, heavy table. Behind it in a Jacobean armchair slouched cool masculinity, in his mid-thirties. He did not bother to rise. Sturdy, long fingers continued to twist the stem of an empty glass.

"Well, Stout, what brings you here?" The rough drawl conveyed lassitude, but the man leaned forwards, his arms resting now on the table. Slate blue eyes gave complete attention to his visitor. "A little something to make you sleep well tonight?"

"Ay, Mr. Rutland. But business first. We have a countertomps here," he ineptly adopted Lady Sarah's foreign word. Mr. Stout was nothing if not quick. "Some of Boney's men, on your land."

He stepped aside to pull forward into the candelabrum's light his suspected spy. "A capital offence, to be out after dark with a blackened face," he announced.

Carefully, as if to a backward child, Lady Sarah protested, "My face is *not* blackened, and it was *not* dark when all this began. We are just trying to reach Ludbury."

Jack Rutland's lower lip, fuller than the upper one, jutted into a wry expression at sight of the nicely curved figure dwarfed by the monstrous hat. An excellent way to attract attention. Ludbury, she said.

"And you suggest we hang her?" he questioned Derby W. Stout.

"Well—uh."

"I will admit my face is stained blue, but . . . " Lady Sarah summoned the blood of her ancestors in order to attain for her modest height a queenly presence. "It is an ancient British custom."

Two blue faces in one day? Jack Rutland slowly dislodged his lean strength from the antique armchair and walked around the table to loom over Stout's saucy spy. "You are—?"

"I am M—," she hesitated, refusing to be intimidated, but trembling at his nearness and the faint smell of sweat from the open neck of his shirt. He lacked an inch or two of Edward's height. "I am Mrs. Smith. And this is my . . . father," she turned to introduce her father-in-law.

"How do you do," the clergyman nodded courteously. "I am anxious to get to bed, if you will show me to my room."

With two fingers, Jack Rutland tilted the wide brim of the spotted hat and ducked his head in order to peer under it at the blue face in question. Was this waif friend to Trimmer's reincarnated volcano with a cast-off from the Celestial Bed in tow? Rutland had not missed her hesitations in the introductions. Father, indeed! Keeping his nightshirt handy to try *her* cure, was he? Well, let him. Tonight Jack Rutland was too tired to spit—and hungry. God, he was starving! But another night, Mrs. . . . . Smith. A handy name, Smith, if you were not what you claimed to be.

As carefully as Jack Rutland studied her face, Lady Sarah scrutinised his. It was a strong face, square-jawed. Golden brown hair, sun-streaked, curled slightly just below his ears. He half smiled at her while he addressed the deputy constable.

"Ah, Stout. I commend your vigilance, but in this case you have been a bit overzealous. Her face is definitely blue rather than black, and I see no criminal intent."

At last, a man of sense! This could well mark the end of the mess she had rushed into. Through Lady Sarah's exhausted body swept a relief as strong as the massive table on which she leaned. She closed her eyes against the glow from the silver candelabrum and shook her head to eliminate the buzz of a hundred angry bees. Did she hear someone say she had fainted? She had not but could not speak to correct the impression. Someone held her, briefly. How comforting, the strength of the arms.

"Could you get rid of the bees?" she asked politely, when she had regained her voice what seemed an instant later.

=9=

"MRS. SMITH. MRS. Smith."

The raspy edge to the male voice kindled alertness. Lady Sarah would not open her eyes until she could identify the voice, and the knuckles rubbed gently against her cheek.

"Sarah?"

Her father-in-law. She opened her eyes to see his anxious face peering from behind the shoulder of the disturbing masculine figure who now leaned back against the side of the long table.

"Hello." His was the voice with the raspy edge. Amusement lurked behind the faint smile and in eyes the blue of northern seas. She remembered those slate blue eyes and where she was.

"Oh, good, Sarah. I would have been worried if I thought you had fainted. I cannot like confusion," her father-in-law fretted.

Lady Sarah looked around at impenetrable blackness, except for the circle of light which held the three of them. Her fingers began to explore crevices in the carved wooden arms of the chair where she sat, her knees almost touching the self-assured male who so closely regarded her.

Had his been the fingers brushing against her cheek? She wished he . . . She closed her eyes at the rush of tears scalding her face. It was shameless to be so starved for a man's attention.

"That bad, eh? To realise the comfortable inn you and your father hoped for is naught but a burnt-out ruin, with only one ramshackle fellow at hand," the distinctive voice teased.

"Kindly allow me to wallow in self-reproach," Lady Sarah retorted, eyes still closed. His laughter prompted her to open them and observe his pleasure in her quick response and the brevity of her bout with tears.

She sighed. "I have made such a mess of things."

"Have you, then? I thought it was my doing, but if you want to claim credit . . . "

He inclined his head at the disarray on the table top, littered with papers, a few books, tattered issues of the *Farmers Magazine*, an empty glass.

How good of him to banter, dispelling any latent threat in his dark lair. Grey eyes met deep blue ones in recognition of peace between them.

"I have no desire to encroach on your rights, sir."

"A pity, because I was hoping you did." His eyes swept the room's boundaries. "God knows I need someone to do a little encroaching around here. I don't suppose you cook?"

"You are hungry?"

"Famished. And the cook dead." Did the gleam in his eyes challenge her assumption of safety in this isolated spot?

"Poisoned? Or overworked?"

He nodded his head. "Both, probably. After almost eighty years, Old Mag drank one too many jugs of cider. Happened some weeks ago, so there is nothing worth foraging for in the kitchen. I do not need a cook so much as a miracle worker."

"I believe those men who led us here will bring food." Featherstone Smith prated his usual optimism.

"Unfortunately, no. The conscientious Stout and his assistant left to resume guard against invasion in the heart of the Midlands."

"Sarah." The vicar turned to his major source of comfort and information, aside from his Bible. "Do you recall when last we ate? I find myself surprisingly hungry."

"I, too, but our host—"

"But Jack Rutland has not paid attention recently to his supply lines. Nevertheless, a clever woman might find in the larder something this poor male has overlooked." He stared directly at Lady Sarah. "You have not denied culinary expertise."

"No, I have not. Do you press me into service?"

"I suspect you are up to volunteering," Jack Rutland grinned, "if you are at all hungry."

"I will volunteer."

For good food from your cook, oversee from experience—more of her mama's indoctrination—summoning memories of spicy cloves and cinnamon in Plumb's steamed puddings, the crusty moistness of the outside slice of a well-basted fowl, a sweet parsnip cake. She could have used Plumb's help tonight, in Jack Rutland's kitchen!

He escorted the Smiths through the ballroom's double doors and back into the summer night. On the other side of the wing, they descended to a ground floor kitchen under the ruins of the dwelling. When lamps were lit, the rough stone walls and uneven floor affirmed years of use.

"Welcome to the thirteenth century. When Old Mag was sober, there was none better at keeping this relic in good order."

A modern cast-iron stove, well polished, stood against the smoke-blackened wall next to a large fireplace complete with roasting spit, tripod with kettle, and various other accoutrements of the up-to-date mediaeval kitchen. Featherstone Smith immediately appropriated a battered wooden armchair—looking old enough to have been the throne of Eleanor of Aquitaine at least, if not Ethelred the Unready—and positioned it to where he could watch the pot on the tripod, should that be necessary.

In the centre of the room, a second wooden armchair, mate to the first, was pulled up to a crudely constructed wooden table. Its scoured top bore the marks of many a knife and cleaver. A ham bone, picked clean, forlorn on a battered pewter platter, was the only item of food in sight. Near it, a tarnished silver epergne with one bent leg tilted crazily.

"And here is the larder." Rutland led Lady Sarah into its close confines. "There was a time when I was a master at foraging," he explained, as together they investigated bins and crocks on the shelves, baskets on the floor. "No chicken coop, nor apple orchard, nor turnip field was safe—"

He turned abruptly, bumping into Lady Sarah, her face lifted towards his. Her slim hands met the warmth of his chest through his thin linen shirt as she braced herself against the impact. Rutland hung there, disciplining his hands to hold to the shelf on each side of the shadowed closet while he looked down on those beautifully formed features.

"None of it safe . . . from my quick fingers." For a long moment, the two shared the same compulsion to remain as they were. He would have taken it further in spite of the old man sitting by the fireplace, but she was a guest, a distraught guest, and Rutland already knew there was more to their mutual accord than could be satisfied by intimacy on a rough pantry floor. He wanted her, but he could wait. In the interests of maintaining their tenuous peace pact, he reestablished the mundane.

"So, what can you report regarding supplies"

"We have turnips and carrots. A few apples and cabbage."

Lady Sarah now feared the immediate future, and wondered about the strength of her will. What was happening to her? She must remember who she was.

Edward's wife, though she suddenly had difficulty envisioning his face. An earl's daughter, bred to honour. Hastily she rummaged through receptacles near the open door to the kitchen.

"Onions!"

"I assume there are also potatoes." The real danger dissipated, Rutland advanced, wanting his raillery to comfort where his arms did not—yet.

"Potatoes, too."

"Oh, well done." Strange what looking into grey eyes the color of smoke, set in that face the color of sky, had done for his exhaustion. She definitely possessed curative powers to equal the Celestial Bed.

He stood too close behind her, thought a quaking Lady Sarah, wondering if her extreme vulnerability resulted from excessive hunger. Were he to wrap his arms about her she would be lost, a victim to anyone offering solid comfort. From the shelf, she grabbed an empty basket as a buffer between them when she turned around. She took breath to still a quavering voice.

"Are eggs and milk nearby?"

"Not near enough. I told you I needed a miracle. If only our parson could conjure up some loaves and fishes."

"If you will fire up the stove, and turn your wine to water," she snapped, balance restored between head and heart. She kicked at a keg that rested under the shelves.

"Careful, or Old Mag will come back to haunt you."

"Looloo. Oh, Looloo," Featherstone Smith called out in the empty kitchen.

Lady Sarah threw a disturbed look at Jack Rutland before going to her father-in-law's side. "Father, you know your Looloo is gone from us." She rubbed her hand over the back of his shoulders. "On the last day of the last century."

Her calm voice soothed the frown from his forehead. The turmoil in his eyes disappeared, and he could smile at the known quantity in his world. "Oh, yes." His hands held on to her forearm. "This big fireplace reminds me of the first place we lived, right after our marriage. Do you remember it, Sarah?"

"No."

"No, of course not. Well, it was so big and so old. Cold, too. In the winter. We moved our bed into the kitchen." He kept his hold on his daughter-in-law's arm and chuckled.

Jack Rutland started the stove fire and brought in the water. Perhaps the old man *was* her father. Certainly, he did not seem to aspire to any Celestial Bed.

Nor did *she* belong there. Instead, her behaviour gave evidence of a privileged background as she improvised with grace and humour in his poorly stocked kitchen. What ill fortune had brought her to involvement in Trimmer's farce?

"I think this ham bone can still serve us," said Lady Sarah, examining it from all angles.

"Surely you jest?"

"No. If it is boiled a little, we can salvage a few scraps for seasoning."

"Let me take charge of the salvage operation," said a skeptical Jack Rutland, confiscating the platter.

"Looloo's mother was horrified that we would have a bed in the kitchen. Like some crofter's cottage, she said. Looloo told her . . . "

"What? What did Looloo say, Father?" asked Lady Sarah, peeling turnips and chopping onions.

He scowled. "I do not remember. Oh, but it was a sweet time, Sarah. A sweet time. For the two of us."

A blend of familiar smells soon added to the contentment that coiled around the occupants of the ancient room and rose with the steam from the stove. Lady Sarah, sleeves rolled up, spooned drippings from the crock on the stove into a skillet where she browned onions before adding them to turnips and potatoes soaking up the remainder of the water into which they had cooked. As she beat the mixture with all her might, curling wisps of hair loosened from her classic coiffure to frame a face glistening with tiny beads of perspiration.

"We would sit in that bed and I would read to her, while the embers crackled. *Robinson Crusoe*. We liked *Robinson Crusoe*." Featherstone Smith extended his visit to the past.

"Your ham, madam." Rutland proffered his two hands, cupped to hold a small pink mound of scraps.

"Oh, well done, Mr. Rutland. Put it in that skillet there." She pointed to the one where the onions had browned, then tasted the results of her exertion from mixing potatoes and turnips.

"Umm. What do you think?" She offered Rutland her spoon, heaped with creamy white flecked with golden bits of onion.

He grasped her wrist, pulling it and the spoon towards him before he tasted her offering. His tongue retrieved a residue from his upper lip as the expectant face before him waited for a favourable verdict.

"Oh, well done, Mrs. Smith," and the two laughed at the foolishness of a phrase so quickly established as part of their rapport.

While he still held her wrist, his eyes locked with hers where triumph flashed. It pleased him to see her happy. "You are a miracle worker," he growled and released her, "but take care not to become so indispensable to me, you may never reach—Ludbury, is it?"

"Did I smell lilacs by the ballroom door?" Lady Sarah asked, both dreading and delighting in his interest.

"I will bring you some. Will we be eating them, too?"

"No, unless you want to skin them."

They had to look away, unable to share further discovery of a deepening compatibility, but affection's warmth merged with the smells and vapours in the room to create an island of great comfort in the essentially grim darkness of Lord Gaunt's ruined abode.

Lady Sarah began to stir slices of pale green cabbage with the ham fragments in a small amount of the drippings. Gradually she added apple slices and thin strips of carrots.

"We were as isolated there in that bed as Crusoe and Friday."

"But surely happier, Father."

Gently he nodded his agreement. A sweet, sweet time. " 'More things belong to marriage than four bare legs in a bed.' Someone wrote that." He began to hum a snatch of old song.

"Now, to add a little water, cover, and cook for a short time," she advised Rutland, who, returning, stood next to her.

"What would happen if we added wine instead?" Rutland appropriated her spoon to stir the skillet's contents.

"Do!" she encouraged. "Be daring." She crossed the room and opened various small drawers in the dresser on the opposite wall. "What if Christopher Columbus had not dared?"

"True. Or 'Turnip' Townshend."

" 'Turnip' Townshend?" Lady Sarah interrupted her search.

"We eat better today, thanks to his daring in agriculture."

"Looloo was ever more daring than I. Ned is so like her."

"Robert Bakewell is another." Rutland dribbled more wine over the cabbage-apple combination.

"Aha!" Lady Sarah communicated victory from the spice drawers, then moved to share with her father-in-law. "Does this smell like cloves?" She held a powdered substance in her palm.

He sniffed. "Faintly spicy."

"Your opinion, sir." She returned stoveside, to Rutland.

"Umm." Her soft palm brushed his cheek as he bent to test the odour. "Old Mag's cooking skill did not carry her far. Whatever it is, it is old, and might well be one of her potions. An emetic we could endure. An aphrodisiac we might not be able to handle. Best throw it out."

He covered the skillet and leaned against the fireplace wall, arms folded against his chest. "We are now going to test whether or not a watched pot boils," he commented to Featherstone Smith, who nodded in solemn understanding of the role of the naturalist in establishing truth.

Rutland watched Lady Sarah as she arranged pale purple lilac blossoms among a small pyramid of green apples on the tarnished silver epergne. Nature's beauty transcended the tarnish and the tilt, adding distinction to the end of the table where they allayed their hunger.

"I have never dined in such style, my lady," Rutland asserted. His hand toyed with a lavender blossom, his conjectures concerning privileged status in her past confirmed.

"Nor I. This is excellent wine, sir," Featherstone Smith had found his way back to the present, "Though there is not much of it," he confided to his daughter-in-law.

How quickly happiness could appear in the midst of disaster, thought Lady Sarah, feeling more kindly about crossing her Rubicon at Camford. "I would like to propose a toast," she announced. "To Plumb, for guiding me through kitchen mysteries."

"By all means, we must toast Plumb," Rutland concurred.

"To Plumb," they chorused.

"To 'Turnip' Townshend," Lady Sarah next proposed, "to whom, I understand, we owe this bounty. Why?"

"Because his successful experiments in agriculture eliminated the waste of letting land lie fallow. We produce more food than before from the same amount of land." Rutland led the salute. "To Lord Townshend."

"And Robert Bakewell? What did he do?"

"Improved the breeding of livestock. More meat on the

bone. He, my lady, though he has been dead for ten years, is going to help build my house. A comfortable, handsome house."

"How, Mr. Rutland?"

"Bakewell could get one thousand guineas for the let of a breeding ram. I now have a comparable ram, and expect it to contribute immensely to my building fund."

"I was very pleased with the contributions to our building fund, for repair of the vestry."

"I am glad to hear that, sir. Now, *I* would propose a toast. To Lord Gaunt, who, in ravaging this pile, failed to burn down the kitchen and ballroom, the very rooms where good food and good company flourish. Never more than tonight." Jack Rutland raised his glass to each of his guests. "Lord Gaunt.

"Mrs. Smith. You do not join our toast."

"He burned down your house!"

"He did, even though I had won it from him in an honest card game."

"You *won* it gambling?"

"Do you know a better way?" His wry smile, dominated by the jutting lower lip, hid the pain of lean years. "Yes. I won my Chance. You said yourself 'be daring.' You heard her, Mr. Smith."

"Yes. I did. I do remember, Sarah." From the depths of his pleasure with the kitchen and the company, the clergyman willingly agreed.

"My final fling at the card table, Sarah. And though Gaunt burned the mansion, he could not destroy pasture, timberland, the river. The estate thrives."

Rutland leaned closer. "Tomorrow, I will show you my Chance."

She thought she could feel the heat of his breath blow in her ear with the words of his invitation. Tomorrow? Tomorrow they *must* leave for Ludbury. Even with hunger satisfied, she was drawn to this vibrant man. She dare not stay too long in his company, not if she was to remember her marriage vows.

The happiness that filled her being as they had cooked together was now tempered, but she would long remember a night that started so grim and ended so unexceptionable.

═10═

WHAT WAS THAT?

Lady Sarah, instantly awake, sat up to survey the bare room. There was no sound save the creak from ropes that supported a straw mattress rustling each time she shifted in the primitive bed.

She rubbed a cheek chafed by the coarse cotton of the mattress cover and, in stockinged feet, padded across warped floorboards to lean out the room's only window. In the pale light of a day barely begun, she could see water glisten below and beyond the ancient manor house where Jack Rutland had provided shelter for the night. How refreshing it would be to bathe in that river's lazy current!

It was impossible to see the wrecked mansion from here, but she could detect no sign of life anywhere. Given this passion for a bath, and obscure light till sunrise, if she hurried—

Out of clothing worn since yesterday morning, she donned Queen Boadicea's limp robe and slipped past the other room of the solar, which held the soft snores of her father-in-law. She paused atop the outside staircase to gaze across a grassy expanse at the ballroom's double doors, still open wide.

Within the dark interior, she could discern no flash of Jack Rutland's white shirt nor glimpse of the rugged length of him but refused to acknowledge any disappointment. She manoeuvred her way cautiously down crumbling steps, then scurried back on an almost invisible path in the direction of the river.

The shock of the cold water stunned. She thrashed and twisted to escape the chill punishment until, gradually, it turned to liquid satin, soothing every inch of her bare skin. She submerged up to her nose and blew bubbles while admiring the rich green of wooded hills on the far side of the river valley. In the light of day, her string of bad decisions did not seem so disastrous.

"There are worse things than sleeping on hay," she defended herself to shrubbery on the bank and blew more bubbles. Much worse. "I shall continue to make decisions because eventually, I will make a good one. In addition . . . "

In addition, what? By daylight, her attraction to Jack Rutland did not seem as overwhelming as it had the night before. The extraordinary feeling of belonging in his kitchen, at one with him, was merely the aftereffect of these past few ghastly days.

She sank below the water's surface as if to drown the memory, her hair streaming out to follow the current, then propelled herself upwards to inhale the fresh morning air spiced with a scent of pine from the hills beyond.

Not so ghastly, really. She and her father-in-law had survived intact. This wild attraction to Jack Rutland, bursting on her like cannon fire, was childish. She had made her choice ten years ago and, in honour, would not forget it. Her host did need someone, however, to see to his creature comforts while he built his home. Perhaps her housekeeper Crippen might recommend a likely candidate—a sensible, experienced woman, mature, used to a straw mattress, and immune to his blandishments.

To the east, the summer sky turned from pearly grey to pale blue. Decisiveness in place, Lady Sarah raced the sun back to the old manor house and had completed her toilet when sunrise burnished the hilltop structures in their varying stages of ruin.

Quietly she entered the ballroom. "Mr. Rutland?"

Wet hair pulled back accentuated the beautiful curves and planes of her face, a fainter blue this morning—the elegant construction of nose, the arch of eyebrows. She wore the dark blue printed cotton.

"Good morning," she said.

Her radiance left him speechless as he looked up from the cluttered table where he worked. He stood immediately, appreciation lighting his keen eyes above well-spaced cheekbones.

"My Lady Sarah. Never say a good night's sleep is not possible on a straw mattress. Your presence this morning gives it the lie." He shielded his eyes. "Or is it the sun, rising in the west this morning, that dazzles me?"

How could she have forgotten the pull of his firm voice, humour softening the roughness of it?

"I rested well, thank you."

"As I noted when I looked in earlier. Gratifying to see both you and your father sleeping so soundly."

Disconcerted, Lady Sarah repeated, "When you looked in on us?"

"Yes. I had the watch. The duty can be yours tomorrow night."

Her crooked smile distorted the perfection of her face, making it less elegant but even more appealing. "Alas, sir, I plan to desert today.

"Desert? when I need your help in restoring order here? how can you plan such action?"

"A cruel nature, sir." She walked past him to look through one of the bank of windows overlooking the river valley. "I bathed in your river this morning."

"I know."

She turned to ask sharply, "You know?" Had he seen her? Watched her?

"Your wet hair. The back of your gown is damp below the neck. What other conclusion should I draw? Are you concluding you were the victim of a Peeping Tom?"

"No, though I would not put it past you."

Rutland laughed. "I may be *de trop*, but not depraved." Even in the clear light of day, this woman was still for him. "You will be pleased to know we are relieved of kitchen duty this morning."

"Oh?"

"I sent Stable John to fetch his married sister. She will rescue us with the kind of food you have a right to expect in the country—not that last night's repast wasn't memorable."

He would not move close to her, but slouched against the table top, his aristocrat's hands resting on its edge. He was content to watch her slender finger idly mark the grime of one window pane.

"It was memorable for me, for us, too." She squared her shoulders and looked at him. "But we must be on our way."

"I confess to disappointment. Can you be persuaded to stay?"

She shook her head, unsure of her ability to reply forcefully in the negative.

"Do you expect me to accept one shake of the head when I have already started to count on your assistance? I thought you could start by training a cook."

"It was more than one shake of the head. It was two or three, which I consider a determined refusal."

"Halfhearted, at best. I won these holdings at cards and am prepared to try my luck again. Are you interested?"

"I thought you said you had not played since winning your estate."

"I have not, but I did not say I was abstinent. Are you game to let a cut of the cards decide the future?"

"No. I will not gamble on that."

"Afraid?" he whispered.

"Yes. I am afraid that you would not win." Her dancing grey eyes belonged in the ballroom setting. "You know I must go."

"No, I do not, but if that is what you wish."

His eyes never left hers, finding satisfaction in her ambivalence. The game was not over.

"Yes. And I count on your help, if you will."

"Certainly. After breakfast?"

"Fine. Most kind of you. You have been so amiable to us in our hour of need."

"My pleasure, of course. I can imagine with what eagerness your family and friends await your arrival in— I believe you said Ludbury."

"Yes. Ludbury is our immediate destination." She began a slow amble around the room, stopping only a moment where trunk and canvas cot occupied an alcove probably designed to hold musicians. "I know you said that with the estate productive and tenants' needs seen to, you could turn your attention to your own comfort. I would really like to help you, to return your kindness, but I believe it is impossible."

"I see that. A young woman, barely chaperoned. A known spy. There will be talk. You can count on Deputy Constable Stout."

"Oh, people talk no matter what one does," she discounted.

Is that why she wore a wedding ring, as did many a spinster, for freedom against gossip since her only other shield was the nominal protection of her feeble father?

Her investigation of the room complete, Lady Sarah crossed back to the window. "You are to be commended for dealing with tenant requirements before your own."

"Thank you. I appreciate your commendation and presume it excuses me for offering you such rough quarters last night."

She glanced about, seeming to calculate the room's dimensions. "What kind of house were you proposing?"

"Nothing grand, but with every modern convenience."

"I imagine you know that the chambre pot has been made obsolete."

"Yes. Definitely."

"I hope you will plan a kitchen close to the dining-room. There is nothing worse than cold food, and so few builders take that into consideration." She had moved closer, earnestly pleading the cause of a convenient kitchen. She halted. "If you value hot food at table, that is."

"I do, very much. It is the kind of advice that I appreciate. Perhaps you could write me your ideas as they occur to you—from wherever you settle."

Lady Sarah could see the laughter in his eyes threaten to spread over the sober mien of his craggy face. She responded to this perception with her own secret smile.

"Do you work early every morning or only on those days when you have the watch?" she enquired, glancing past him to the riot of papers on the table.

He turned to share her view. "The damnable accounts. Like the poor, always with us." Regarding her wearily, he commented, "I don't suppose you can do accounts."

She turned away from him and looked to the doorway. "I must check on my father-in—"

His hand grabbed her shoulder. "You *do* accounts!" he exclaimed. "It is therefore your sacred duty—as one beleaguered human to another—to stay when you are so well qualified to help me."

She was rigid under his touch. His poor lost lamb. A gentlewoman saddled with a retired clergyman for a father must fight a continuing battle against poverty—and importuning males. If she did not take to the streets, she took whatever she could to keep starvation at bay. Probably on their way now to some distant relative who would parsimoniously begrudge them every mouthful they might consume.

"I tell you what, Mrs. Smith." He spoke earnestly, holding both her shoulders, willing her to realise her future lay at Chance. "The completion of sheepshearing has added another bale of papers to the mountain already here. Stay long enough to reduce the mountain to a molehill, and I will personally escort you to Ludbury, or wherever you want to go. In return, while you are here, you will have good food and lodging—such as it is—for you and your father, and wages. What would be fair?"

Her look warned him away as she drew back. He released her immediately.

Insouciance returned to the husky drawl that followed Lady Sarah's trudge towards the double doors leading out to the entry hall.

"If, in addition, Mrs. Smith, I relieve you of any responsibility for the night watch, would you consider staying? My final offer, Sarah."

She held to the door as she turned back towards him. "I find it impossible to refuse your final offer, Jack Rutland." Her smile, too broad to be lopsided, belied the wistful resignation in her voice.

He shook his head. Not even with the high stakes during the card game with Gaunt had Jack felt so drained after winning. Maybe because today's victory was only the first hand to be played, and perhaps the stakes were much higher—the future happiness of them both. Thank God he had a life worth sharing with her.

"I will stay only if no money is involved. I do your accounts. You take us to Ludbury. A strictly business arrangement."

"I would not have it any other way, Mrs. Smith." And every June, year after happy year, they would celebrate the anniversary of Derby W. Stout's intervention in their lives.

=11=

NORTHERN LIGHT FROM the bank of windows at her back silhouetted the neatly organised table top where Lady Sarah hunched over Jack Rutland's accounts. He had exaggerated their mountainous state. Midway through the second day following her arrival at Chance, she was close to bringing order back to his estate office in the ballroom.

In spite of her struggle with addition—eights in particular—it had been interesting to discover the shrewdness concealed within their host's affability. As revealing as the tally of expences were the costs *not* incurred during his disciplined advance on profitability. She would be imprudent to underestimate this man.

More sevens—almost as bad as eights—nineteen and seven were twenty . . . six. Five fingers and two thumbs hit in succession upon the wood grain of the carved oak table.

"You'll be surprised at the increased yield."

Lady Sarah looked up expectantly at the sound of Jack Rutland's voice in the stone-flagged entry hall. She was glad to be coping with his sevens and eights, yet eager for his interruption.

"Dutch ashes, you say." A sturdy farmer accompanied Chance's owner-steward through the double doors. Heavy boots scuffed across the unpolished parquet.

"Yes. Enriches the soil."

"Better than what the good Lord gave us?"

"He helps those who help themselves. Even shines

upon them, as the Reverend Smith would have it."

With studied ease, Rutland introduced the squire and explained Lady Sarah's presence. "During her father's visit, Mrs. Smith applies her mathematical gifts to my accounts."

The bluff man of the soil, uncomfortable in a ballroom regardless of the circumstances, twisted the hat in his hand while he responded to Lady Sarah's smile of greeting.

"Word's all the way to my place, other side of Roundgrove, how Rutland's Chance were exempt from last year's poor harvest. Believe your kinsman knows what he's doing, Mistress Smith, and I'm obliged for his advice."

"I believe it pleasures him to give it." Kinsman?

The isolated estate of two nights ago seemed more like Hyde Park today as a need to consult on modern farming methods burgeoned. Rutland laid the phenomenon at Derby W. Stout's door.

"Been meaning to come for some time." The squire studied Lady Sarah through squinting eyes, as if comparing her against the rumours. "Then, when I heard all that babble from Deputy Constable Stout, I knew today was the day." If he was disappointed in her lack of a blue face, he did not show it.

"Never've seen anyone so taken with his own importance as Derby W. Stout. You'd think he was His Majesty, Farmer George. A stroke of luck, Mistress Smith, that your countertomps with Stout happened so close to your kin."

"We are only distantly related," she murmured, relieved that her face had faded and her back was to the light.

"With close family ties," Rutland elaborated.

"Until the feud," amended Lady Sarah, determined to distance herself from his fabrication.

Eyes alert, the squire anticipated replacing Derby W.

Stout as the centre of conversational circles. His hopes were dashed by Rutland.

"For your father's sake, Mrs. Smith, let us forget the sad past and dwell on a better future. Squire brings word that thirty acres adjoining Chance are coming up for sale. There are orchards and a house. You did say a habitable house?"

"Oh, yes. Small, but sound." He peered to the right and left, absorbing the bare room's deterioration. "I'd say you needed the house more'n the orchards. Gaunt land originally, so by rights it should come to you, I think."

"Worth considering. Gaunt owes me a house. Might be useful to have one now. Mrs. Smith proposes to remove her father's spiritual guidance from us unless better accommodations are provided."

Spiritual guidance, indeed! thought the maligned lady, finally recognising that Rutland, like some wily creature in nature, would protect her by focussing on her father-in-law as the reason for their Chance sojourn.

"House would do for your chaplain," the squire acknowledged. "You'd need somebody here, then, to do accounts."

He stared at Jack Rutland before proceeding. "Daughter does mine. A smart lass."

The man from Roundgrove nodded at Lady Sarah, seeming to share with her the ultimate purpose of his visit. Not just enriched soil involved here. She returned his nod, mischief sparking her soft grey eyes. Here was an advantageous alliance. Notwithstanding the informal appearance—loose shirt open at the throat, faded breeches tucked in worn riding boots—Rutland was the answer to a prospective father-in-law's prayers.

"Make a fine wife for someone wants a hard worker from good family. Mother was a Wyerville."

"But who would do *your* accounts if she were to leave you?" Rutland artlessly enquired before steering his visitor back into agricultural matters.

Having referred to relevant publications stacked in a corner, the pair departed, leaving Lady Sarah to elaborate on the family feud she had invented. She found it difficult to master numbers when Rutland's image impinged on her concentration.

She stood to check the view from the windows, which were sparkling clean, courtesy of Stable John. Across the river valley, forested hills demonstrated every shade of green to a cloudless sky, while just below, the married sister sat shelling peas as she imparted local gossip to Featherstone Smith. That servant of the Lord indiscriminately pulled at herbs and weeds in the overgrown kitchen garden nearby, displaying an agrarian interest only just evident. Perhaps he could aid Rutland with horticultural direction as well as spiritual guidance.

She chuckled over that remote possibility. No. They must leave, she and her father-in-law. Tomorrow, if convenient, or the day after. Regretfully, she eschewed the example of Ulysses' wife Penelope, unravelling the day's work each night. It was just as well. Lady Sarah Smith was in no position to share Jack Rutland's expectations.

Odd, but that was almost the cruellest aspect of Edward's defection—losing not just him, but his aspirations. Was she doomed to lead an aimless existence until his return, another Vauncy Frome will-o'-the-wisping the countryside? She groaned, shaking her head against the awful prospect. And what if Edward never returned? Why relinquish the happiness she had found here? If she earned their keep, where was the harm in prolonging their visit?

> To thine own self be true,
> And it must follow, as the night the day
> Thou canst not then be false to any man.

Her papa had chosen the words from Shakespeare, and she had begrudged every moment spent embroidering them long ago. At last, the exercise seemed worthwhile.

Appropriate advice charging across time.

Back to the account book, a heart solaced, her fingers danced a number count on the table top. Eight shillings to the carter. Two pounds, four shillings for—

"I thought you said you did accounts." Jack Rutland lounged against the door jamb, arms folded across his chest.

"I never said that. You assumed it."

"I do not recall your denial." Arms behind his back, he sauntered across the space that separated them.

"Nothing was said about absolute correctness." She could not keep from laughing when she was in this man's company.

"Are the figures close enough to reality to give me a fair idea of where I stand?"

"Very close."

"Who could ask for more?" he leaned over her shoulder to study the entries in the account book. "And can I afford to acquire additional acres?"

"I cannot answer about income, but this is the most recent expence total."

"I finally retire one mortgage, only to contemplate another."

"Interest rates are low."

"That's so." He did not bother to hide the tenderness in his eyes. Here she sat, dressed for a drawing-room in white embroidery, and brandishing familiarity with interest rates. She was determined to use her wits to survive—and not doing too well at it. Yet, not doing too badly either. His accounts were current. A further glance at the table's orderliness confirmed the worst. She had, in fact, finished the task assigned.

He relaxed against the end of the table. "I have always wanted orchards."

"They are lovely when the trees are in bloom."

"Invariably. I want the property—assuming squire's hearsay is fact, and the house has a kitchen properly placed. Shall we ride over tomorrow to see so you can judge? Your opportunity to see my Chance, too, before our Ludbury trip."

"I would like time to engage a cook before I leave." She hastened to answer his questioning look, sputtering in the process. "Well, I just thought it would be easier to go if I knew you were at least well fed, if not decently housed."

"No need to concern yourself. Enough ale houses about, and gifts of food occasionally make their way to the kitchen."

He answered her raised eyebrows. "There are some who think my advice worth a frumenty or shepherd's pie. Though, come to think of it, it might have been Old Mag's potions that brought in the bounty."

"You see? You should have a cook."

"Who but Old Mag would put up with these living conditions?"

"If you acquire the house with the orchards, then anyone—"

"*If*, Sarah?"

Lady Sarah nodded, pensive. "Of course. It is unwise to rely on hearsay. Perhaps the squire's 'smart lass'—"

"I have other plans."

She answered quickly to overcome a sudden hollow feeling. "So all you can do is hope for continuing appreciation from your tenants and those from neighbouring estates."

"Considering I am about the only landlord at hand, the odds are favourable for enough savoury meals to keep me in good health." He smiled. "A harmonious give and take has taken root here, Sarah."

"Are you Mr. Jack Rutland?"

A tall woman, thin as a shepherd's crook in faded brown cotton, had hesitated in the doorway. Black hair cropped at her ears and a beaked nose gave her face its look of uncompromising severity, but there was uncertainty in her voice and dejection in her pockmarked face.

"With one major exception," Rutland muttered, "and this probably has to do with it."

He stood in welcome and in readiness, if the quaver in the newcomer's voice was indicative of the degree of her despair.

"I am. Please come in."

"They said I should come to you."

Rutland nodded.

"I am Belle Granger, from the mill."

"Miss Granger. This is Mrs. Smith."

"Mrs. Smith."

The quaver had disappeared in response to their courteous reception. Intensely green eyes conveyed her gratitude. She hardly seemed of an age to warrant the cobweb of grey in her wiry black hair.

"It's my father's watch. Bibby Bibbrow's taken it, when it didn't even run, and told me never to come back to the mill. Said I was a troublemaker, with not a word about what a good worker I am." She had refused Lady Sarah's offer of the chair, and stood, arms straight at her side, hands clenched. She turned to Lady Sarah. "We all know he makes the mill clock go faster when we stop to eat, but I wasn't trying to check up on him. Just showing some of the children how to tell time."

Now, she addressed Rutland. "They say you'd be the only one could get it back for me. That watch is all I have left of my family, and it just means all the world to me."

"He took it away thinking you would accuse him of cheating on the meal time due you?" Rutland clarified the motive.

"I imagine, though it's a wonder why I would when he's paying me more money than I can earn most places."

"Do you want to be reinstated at the mill?" Rutland continued his interrogation.

She slowly shook her head. "Watches are forbidden," she admitted, resigned. "I broke the rule, Mr. Rutland.

And once Bibby Bibbrow gets his mind set on a thing, there's no changing it."

What will you do for employment?" asked Lady Sarah, from her heightened concern and first-hand experience at being without funds.

"I'll survive." Belle Granger shrugged her shoulders. "Have for forty years when no one else in my family did." Green eyes questioned slate blue ones. "I don't ask for anything but my father's watch."

"You still work a fourteen-hour shift?"

"More in the summer, when it's light longer."

"So you work—"

"From four in the morning, till ten at night lately."

"Apprentices, too?"

Thick lips broke into a smile, upper teeth projecting slightly over lower ones in appreciation of his line of questioning. "No, sir. You won't get him there. He hasn't indentured anybody since the law made it wrong to work apprentices at night."

Rutland heaved a sigh, his wry smile answering the millworker's. She lost her stern look when she smiled. The green eyes shone, and one could understand why the infant had been named Belle.

"Were you eating better over there?"

"We had some good bacon for a while, but we're back to the rancid meat. I think that's why I got out my watch, to interest the little ones and keep them from fighting the pigs for what was in the trough."

Rutland addressed the pain on Lady Sarah's face. "Bibbrow runs the mill as he sees fit until his long-term lease runs out next year."

"So you cannot retrieve Miss Granger's watch?" Lady Sarah had left her chair to stand beside them.

"Where did you hear that?" he grinned. She was standing too near by far. The clean smell of her assailed him. "This is my week to play knight-errant."

"I want to go with you." Lady Sarah replied instantly.

"The Reverend Mr. Smith, too. The weight of the church must surely be of help."

He stood there, long finger rubbing his chin as he memorised the longing on her face. "No. The less made over this, the better. But I like the offer." He left abruptly, before he was so beyond control as to reach out and let the same finger follow the line of her chin. "I will return with the watch, Miss Granger," he called back.

Under the sweet fragrance of lilac bushes, the two women sat and waited on the steps of the ballroom wing where they could watch the sun's descent towards a line of trees that marked the encircling river beyond. Neither woman partook of the cheese and cider Lady Sarah had brought back from the kitchen.

"Where is the mill, Miss Granger?"

"Downriver, but not far. Not even an hour's walk." She sat stiffly.

"My father-in-law and I have not been here but two days, yet I am certain you can count on Mr. Rutland."

"A fair man, I hear."

"And though it may not be too fine, he will shelter you while you need it." Lady Sarah wondered if any comfort she could offer was worth breaching this woman's self-containment.

"If I can just have the watch, I'll not ask more of him."

"When he returns with it, then what will you do?"

"I may find a place at a mill not far to the north. I'm skilled, and reliable," she spoke with bravado. "Mills are a boon to women who must earn their living. Pay is better than with most things we could do."

"It is a frightening thing to want funds while some stern face insists on money."

Belle studied in surprise the extent of the fervour in one wearing a gown of the finest grade muslin, richly embroidered. Sensing sympathy behind the passion, the spinster conceded more biography.

"After my father died, my mother and I kept his school

for a while."

"You were a *teacher*!" Lady Sarah commented happily. "I tried teaching briefly. History." A scoff issued from Queen Boadicea's blue face, paler today than yesterday.

"We didn't prosper, what with having to support my brother's family as well. He was struggling to establish himself as an attorney. When my mother died, I took the little I'd managed to save and went to live with them." Belle Granger shook her head. "I think maybe the discord killed him. His wife was a flibbertigibbet. Found a new husband almost before the burial service was over. I guess she had to, but I went into the mill."

"Rather than return to teaching?"

"I've none of the airs and graces you need to teach children of the ones who can afford it. When I deal with others, the ones who only know about working one machine their whole lives, then I find trouble. I know Bibby Bibbrow resents me. He thinks I was teaching those women and children to expect more than they've a right to."

"I like children. They are so joyously curious and—" Lady Sarah stopped herself, unwilling to be reminded of her barrenness and spoil this day at Chance.

"Curious, for certain."

"Often I have thought it would be a fine thing to teach little ones."

"Bibbrow's mill is not the place to start." The spinster shivered, and rested her forehead in her hands. The little finger of her left hand was misshapen.

"Were you abused?"

Lady Sarah's query startled the woman until she realised the cause. "Oh, that. Caught in a machine. 'Tis not unusual." With a rough hand she smoothed the fingers of the other, mutilated one. "No. I was just trying to blot out Bibby Bibbrow's little smirk. Comes whenever he's displeased, which is most of the time. I believe I'll be glad to be gone from there."

"Do you cook?" Lady Sarah's managerial propensities surfaced in the continuing effort to bring a solution to the woman's immediate problem. "Mr. Rutland needs someone to cook and look after him."

"I can cook, but not fancy such as he'd want."

"Oh, I cannot think he will require anything but tasty fare."

Belle Granger smiled at the determined young woman. "If I sit here and listen to you long enough, I'll think I can do anything I've a mind to, maybe even jump over the moon."

"Tomorrow you shall march over to the mill and dismiss that Bibby Bibbrow and *you* will run the mill!"

"And *then* I'll jump over the moon!" Belle had to laugh at such absurdity.

"I know just the thing." Lady Sarah ran to the old manor house, returning with the spotted hat. "Here you are. Wear this for your audience with the moon king."

Entranced, the lanky millworker set it atop her unsightly hair and plain face. There, the hat no longer seemed so atrocious.

"Belle, you look quite handsome. You must keep it for good luck in your future."

"But I couldn't."

"Of course you can. If you do not use it for your audience with the man in the moon, then wear it when you sit in the business office of the mill or on your wedding day. We must find a dress to match."

"Mrs. Smith." Belle Granger had no words, but would long remember the afternoon on the steps of the ruined mansion. As the two sat together in companionable silence, she gulped the cider, still cool, and bit into the cheese, creamy and tart. Insects darting among the blue blossoms in a clump of Jacob's Ladder contradicted the general indolence of the afternoon as the wait for the timepiece went on.

"I wonder why Mr. Rutland has not returned." Lady

Sarah regarded the sun drawing near to the line of trees. "I think he has had more than enough time to get to the mill and back. Could he be in danger?"

"Bibby Bibbrow must be approached carefully." Now, it was Belle Granger who sought to comfort.

The sun had hit the trees when Jack Rutland loped up the slight incline from the manor house, whose great hall on the ground floor had long served as stable. He held the watch aloft like a trophy. "Belle Granger, I believe you were missing your watch."

"Sir," she whispered, blinking back tears as she stood in welcome.

He took in the spotted hat with the yard-wide brim. Had the thing found a new owner? His eyes moved on to Lady Sarah's gladsome countenance. It was such a special moment, to have her here at the end of the day, particularly a day requiring negotiations with greed.

"Rutland, you bearded the dragon," she exclaimed with relief, and offered him her untouched cider before backing away to sit again on the steps.

If she would not be false to Edward, she must keep her distance from this man. He returned his attention to the spinster, his jutting lower lip accenting a rueful glance.

"What have you been telling her, Belle Granger?"

"That Bibby Bibbrow is a bully," Lady Sarah snapped, "and as likely to crush a finger as look at you."

Rutland gazed with compassion at the poor drudge in the incongruous hat as he answered Lady Sarah. "Only a bully to the weak, Mrs. Smith. For his landlord, he has nothing but smiles—unctuous smiles, I'll grant you, but smiles nonetheless."

Belle Granger bobbed her head in agreement. "How did you persuade him to return the watch?"

"I appealed to his sense of chivalry."

She snorted. "Whatever you had to give, I'll work it off. I'll not have you in his debt because of me."

Rutland continued on his own tack. "Bibby told me you

were once a teacher," he said, cupping her elbow in his hand and courteously seeing her seated next to Lady Sarah. For his own self-preservation, he dropped down at the other end of the stairstep, removing himself from where he could too easily touch her, trace her lips, the line of her throat. He drew a deep breath and went on.

"I told him he ought to see you as an opportunity to institute some modern management at the mill—at little extra cost. Woollen mills need to enter the nineteenth century along with the cotton mills."

At little extra cost? Miss Granger clutched her watch to her heart. How many years had he pledged her to work at the mill in exchange for her treasure returned? The words "modern management," when Bibby Bibbrow used them, meant work till midnight, and boded ill.

"After he compared last summer's output to the winter's, he saw there was little difference, in spite of increased working hours. I suggested he might achieve an increase if he demonstrated to his workers an interest in their welfare.

"What we finally agreed to, Miss Belle Granger—provided you could be persuaded to return—"

Persuade me to return? The discharged worker could only wonder how much Mr. Jack Rutland was disguising the conversation that actually took place.

"—was an experiment during July, testing whether there is profit in kindness."

The irony in Rutland's rasping voice did not escape Bibbrow's recalcitrant employee, who had begun to pay closer attention.

"The work day will be reduced to winter hours, and, of the forty-minute meal break at midday, twenty will be spent in reading instruction—of a morally uplifting nature, of course. Bibby insisted. At the end of the month and each succeeding one, should it come to pass, he alone will determine whether the program and Miss Belle Granger should continue.

"Teaching will be your responsibility, Belle, for one extra shilling a week. I promised to find someone to help you. Andrew Pebbleship's mother might agree, though she is deaf, come to think of it, and could not hear the students. What do you think?" Rutland would not look at Lady Sarah, though he was aware she had fixed her stare on the setting sun and appeared not to be listening.

Belle Granger shook her head. "You're trying to improve things there, Mr. Rutland, and I thank you. But Bibby Bibbrow agrees to anything you want. Then, as soon as you've turned away, he stops. I believe he sold the food you sent over for us."

"Did he now?" Rutland's noncommittal reply belied the glint in his eyes.

"Yes, sir. He'll blame me for coming to you, but he'll take his anger out on every last one of us. It's fearsome, with none wanting the risk of being let go." The quaking spotted hat emphasised the vigour of her denial.

"Oh, Belle." Lady Sarah reached over to touch the spare figure.

"You thought to encourage me, I know, Mrs. Smith. And I *was* encouraged. Except that . . . " She shook her head again. "Going against Bibby Bibbrow is not worth even the extra shilling."

Slowly she took off the hat and handed it back. "I don't believe I merit this, since I won't be jumping over the moon."

"No! Keep it, Belle. As a good omen."

"I understand the extent of Bibbrow's power over you, Belle, but I cannot accept your fear of it—not when I need your help." Rutland's rough voice soothed. "I negotiated for a teacher during the month of July, and a teacher is what we will have."

Lady Sarah watched his mouth, especially his full lower lip. She felt the power behind his soft appeal to the millworker and the exhilaration beneath the surface of his casual tone. These were enough to make one believe anything was possible where Rutland was involved.

"Mrs. Smith was just saying what a fine thing it is to teach." Belle sought relief from Rutland's persuasive force. "Maybe she should be the one to do it."

Her voice faded to nothing. She looked at Lady Sarah, whose eyes were on the landowner, then smoothed the fingers of her mutilated hand.

"Unfortunately, Mrs. Smith and her father leave tomorrow."

Rutland's eyes lingered over Lady Sarah's aureate form as she sat in the last golden rays of the summer day. When their eyes connected, he could not read what lay in hers. Once the turn of a card had settled his future. Once again, his future depended on chance and this woman's willingness to stay. He didn't care to think of all his tomorrows without her presence.

"Yes, I did say that about teaching."

Eager to fill the empty places in her life with Rutland's plan for the millworkers, Lady Sarah still hesitated, remembering the consequences of her impulsive reaction at The Wise Owl. Had she learned nothing from that? Duty lay at Long Wood. She should return there, as befitted a wife, and wait for Edward to do the same. Yet, where was the harm in a few more days' delay? She *was* going to Long Wood and had been for the past nine days. It was simply taking longer than usual to make the trip. "I think, if Belle is to succeed as your teacher, Mr. Rutland, you need someone helping her who is not at the mercy of Bibby Bibbrow."

"Yes."

He would not push her into the decision. Still, he was having difficulty breathing as he maintained a nonchalance he was far from feeling.

Belle Granger remained unconvinced. "I guess any bravery I had has grown threadbare over the years, Mr. Rutland, or I'd be proud to help you."

"It is fearsome for any of us, Belle, to face unkindness."

The fierce tone of Lady Sarah's comment startled Jack Rutland, his earlier surmise of her situation reenforced as she addressed him from across the width of the shallow stairs. "If I were to delay our journey, *briefly*, to stand guard against your Bibby's bullying tactics, do you think you could find a replacement for me in a very few days?"

"I would make every effort, Mrs. Smith."

"But we'd need paper and ink to make ABC's." Belle conjured another obstacle.

"You shall have them," Rutland pledged.

"Is it possible to buy paints in the village? Bright red, perhaps, and yellow?" Lady Sarah's words tumbled forth as disordered as the ideas crowding her thoughts. "It ought to be easier to learn with coloured letters."

"We will try every village till we find what you want."

Lady Sarah stood and smiled at Rutland. "Then, Mr. Rutland, you have your teacher." She glanced at Belle, daring her to contradict. She did not, as she regarded this new force in her life with considerable awe.

Lady Sarah justified her decision. This was not at all like joining Vauncy Frome at The Wise Owl. She was much better acquainted with Jack Rutland's admirable traits.

"And your terms, Mrs. Smith." He stood, happily breathing deep.

"Yes?"

"I believe ours remains a strictly business relationship."

"It does." Lady Sarah thought a moment. "I, too, have a piece of family jewellery that needs retrieving and could use your help."

"I assume it is not housed in the Tower of London."

She nodded, her eyes gleaming appreciation at his foolish inference.

"Then, if it is to be retrieved honestly, I agree to your terms." He extended his hand.

She took it and lifted her voice in an old melody. *"If*

buttercups buzz'd after the bee, if boats were on land, chur-ches on sea." Still holding his hand, she pulled him down the steps and began a country dance around his fixed stance. "*If summer were spring, and the other way 'round, then all the world would be upside down.*" She stopped. "Mr. Rutland. Belle. Let us turn the world upside down."

"Mrs. Smith," said Rutland. "You already have."

He swung her slim body in as wide an arc as had not been seen since the second Henry Tudor took to the dance floor.

July

=12=

"Looks as if the Lord don't mean for millhands to read," Balthasar Bibbrow commented to workers and well-wishers assembled in the transient stillness of the large workroom. Bibby Bibbrow, never called that to his face, stood under the wall clock with his watch in hand and gazed with satisfaction at the sudden rain shower outside and the disquieted faces within.

"Three minutes gone already," announced the reluctant supporter of education for the masses, whose every utterance was foretold by a drone.

Of Rutland's height, but fleshy, the lessee of the mill flaunted the power he enjoyed over the eighty cowed creatures hovering by machines that carded and spun. His pale blue eyes, deep set, darted along each row, worker by worker, before assaulting the quartet of outsiders. Dark hair singed grey was worn in the style of the last century, and offered a clue to the extent of his adherence to such good old-fashioned ways as serfdom and the cucking stool.

"Five minutes, now." His smug proclamation dared rebuttal.

Rutland regrouped his teaching force, made ill at ease by the constraints of the situation. Jettisoning their plan for outdoor schooling, he assisted the Reverend Mr. Featherstone Smith to mount a wooden box, from which elevated position the vicar requested the Almighty to look with favour upon the inaugural occasion.

The aging minister, never stronger than when he was delivering a sermon, took inspiration from the downpour to launch the story of Noah, while Lady Sarah used the time to improvise additional learning devices. Rutland interrupted the long catalogue of animals marching two by two, motioning to her to replace the vicar atop the makeshift speaker's stand.

"This is an A," lady Sarah held up the sheet with the green letter, "the first letter of the alphabet." Raising it higher, she made sure every worker saw it before handing it to Belle, who stuck it in the red band of her spotted teaching hat. It leaned against the high crown. "A."

Lady Sarah held one of the new placards. "And this is the word *ark*, that Noah built for all the animals. Who can find an A in this word?"

Absolute silence greeted the invitation, except for the sough of the rain. All looked to Bibby Bibbrow's intimidating presence. He blocked the doorway to his office behind Lady Sarah, daring anyone to answer.

"This is the *A* in the word *ark*, Noah's ark." She pointed to the correct letter on the placard and to the one tucked in Belle's hat. "*A*".

The senior Mrs. Pebbleship, counting herself a recruit by dint of the loan of her watercolour paints, was particularly proud of her word placard, having spent most of yesterday afternoon on it. *Teacher* had been painted in bright yellow and outlined in black. Red flowers decorated the border. Short and stout in the black bombazine of widowhood, she handed the product of her artistic leanings to the beleaguered instructor.

If the round, little matron resembled a currant in the room's sombre mix, Lady Sarah was the citron in the cambric morning dress with raised collar and elbow-length sleeves. Only a hint of blue dye tinted her face as she tried again.

"This is the word *teacher*. I am your teacher. Who can

find an *A* in this word?"

Silence again prevailed, though close attention was given the colourful representation.

Next, the uneasy students were introduced to the word card *clean*. "You keep your machines clean." Jack Rutland, more aware of the politics of commerce, had suggested this example.

"Polly, can you find an *A* in the word *clean*? I know how hard you try to keep your machine clean." Bravely, Belle Granger sought to further their cause.

Polly studied her employer, the word card, the floor. Lady Sarah, still holding the card high, jumped down from the up-ended wooden box to move along the side of the room.

All eyes followed the shift, which excluded Bibby Bibbrow from the background. Belle tugged at deaf Mrs. Pebbleship's sleeve. With word cards held high, they joined their colleague.

"Come point to a letter that looks exactly like the one stuck in Belle Granger's hat," Lady Sarah coaxed. "Do come, Polly, and find an *A*."

"Rose, help her." Belle's determination grew with Lady Sarah's failure to win converts.

Everyone watched the two girls as hand in hand they shuffled towards Lady Sarah's expectant face.

"Wat! You come, too," Belle urged.

Emboldened by the safe progress of the others, the child strutted towards the centre of scholastic endeavour. Cautiously, the three workers dared point to the *A* in each word card.

"Good for you." Lady Sarah crowed in relief.

The trio peeked at the storm clouds gathering on Bibby Bibbrow's brow as Jack Rutland added his praise. Eager to consolidate success, Lady Sarah whisked into Belle's other hand the makeshift word card that spelled *rain*.

"Where is the *A* in this word?" the suffering teacher demanded of the three, torn between basking in further praise or suffering Bibby Bibbrow's future ill will.

The opportunity to star proved impossible to resist, and they repeated their previous victory, identifying the *A* in the new word.

Lady Sarah risked more silence. "Who can guess what this word says? What is outside the mill today?"

"Pigs!" Wat jumped at the chance to shine.

"Heaven!" shouted Rose with unrestrained joy.

Belle was more specific. "What falls from the sky to get us wet when we go outside?"

"Rain!" Caught up in the suspence, Lady Sarah blurted out the answer, then clapped her fingers to her mouth. An anxious business, to fight the silence and spark interest from out of the gloom.

"Well done," said Jack Rutland.

He winked at her, restoring her equanimity with their pre-arranged signal. Bibby Bibbrow must have no cause to complain at the duration of their incursion.

"It is time to go," she rejoined the mill master, "but we will come tomorrow, with more *A*'s and some *B*'s and maybe even a *C*," she promised those assembled. "Before we leave, we would like to honour," she gulped, "the one who made today's meeting possible." Trained to preserve a serene countenance regardless, Lady Sarah's smile dazzled and must surely have once contributed to her husband's notice by his superiors. "Mr. Bibbrow, would you mark our beginning with a few words?"

Slowly, ponderously, Bibby Bibbrow transferred his bulk from the office doorway, a complacent little smile bridging his large cheeks. "Back to work," he ordered, with perhaps a trace of civility not detected by the unschooled ear.

The whir of old machinery replaced the rain's now intermittent spatter. Jack Rutland conspicuously observed the amenities with both Bibby Bibbrow and Belle Granger before ushering his party out into a dripping world. Warm air hung heavy with moisture as they crossed the mill yard to follow the track by the river.

"I thought it went quite well." Featherstone Smith spoke from a lifetime stance of unrealistic calculations. Water droplets accumulating on his black coat hardly seemed to warrant the hurried pace his daughter-in-law tried to induce.

"I wish we could better working conditions." Disappointment nourished Lady Sarah's impatience with her father-in-law's imperturbability. Why didn't things go right from the very start?

"In due time, Mrs. Smith," Rutland counselled.

"We never even got to the B's," lamented Mrs. Pebbleship, accepting his assistance over slippery ground.

"Not easy to light the lamp of learning in the dark shadow of Bibbrow's smile." Jack Rutland struggled—half tugging, half pulling—to speed the plump Pebbleship along a path grown treacherous. It had begun to spit rain again lightly.

"I was certain there would be time for the B's." Unable to hear him, the matron persisted, panting from the exertion of their walking speed, "And my sign for *bread* . . . so clever . . . I think you agreed . . . Mrs. Smith."

Lady Sarah smiled back over her shoulder and nodded. In the drizzle, curling wisps escaped her smooth coiffure to fall over her eyes, hindering a view of the way. She stumbled, and would have pulled down her father-in-law but for Rutford's steadying hand from behind.

The yellow cambric gown in its limp state achieved the height of London fashion, clinging to her every curve and heartening a Jack Rutland at toil with Mrs. Pebbleship's less than sure foot. He had shed his coat to protect her black bombazine, and his chest and arm muscles glistened through a soaked shirt.

They took shelter from further drenching under a limestone ledge just past the river's upper falls, where water rushed along divers courses across descending levels of rock shelves to spill foam in scattered pools. Bobbing leaves on surrounding greenery attested to the rain's steady insistence.

"Do we visit Neptune, Sarah?" said the Reverend Mr. Smith, his voice raised above the water music and the rain's rustle of foliage. He swung his hat and brushed moisture from his coat sleeves. "I suggest we made a wrong turn and have arrived at the bottom of the sea."

"And how beautiful it is, Father. Is there a romantic name for this place, Mr. Rutland?" Lady Sarah sought his attention over the heads of their elders, the hum of the water. Hard not to focus on his flesh glowing through the wet linen.

"The Upper Falls," he answered with a grin. He had managed to redirect Mrs. Pebbleship's motherly efforts to dry him with her shawl towards the clergyman, who welcomed her ministrations.

"How disappointing. Such a scene would be called . . . um . . . " Lady Sarah searched her vocabulary.

"The Bride's Falls," her father-in-law declared above the sounds of cascading water.

"More like the bride's lace petticoat, parson," Jack Rutland refined, laughing at Lady Sarah's damp disorder. How much he was attracted to every aspect of her, "her infinite variety" as Shakespeare would have it. Cook, bookkeeper, teacher—he wondered at her next role. Wife.

"What besides *bread* should we use for the *B*'s?" Andrew Pebbleship's mother enthused over the prospect of a steady audience for her artwork. She dived into creative thought, deeply so because of her deafness, and temporarily lost touch with her companions.

"*Bride* has a *B*," Rutland's teasing eyes found the hollow in Lady Sarah's throat, just perceptible between the collar lines of her yellow dress. "And *bed*. One illustration could do for both words. Admirable," his eyes travelled downwards, "efficiency."

"*Beware* has a *B*," Lady Sarah volleyed.

"But not needed here, Mrs. Smith. I suggest you serve as illustration if the Pebbleship does portraits. Even in your *bedraggled* state . . . you are a sight to *behold*."

"And you, a veritable fountainhead for the letter, Mr. Rutland!"

"*Behold*, the *beautifully bedraggled bride* in the *bed* Should do it, Mrs. Smith. Which brings us to the *C*'s. Who is *caressing* the bride in the bed?"

"Someone who *cares* for her deeply, I hope. Someone who is *committed*, for ever," Lady Sarah lashed out, unthinking. She looked away, unable to bear Rutland's suddenly fierce stare, not wanting him to witness the hurt she feared had surfaced in her eyes, but he had seen her pain and proceeded with caution, wishing he could keep those grey eyes trouble free always.

"Our bride, Mrs. Smith . . . our bride is joined to a man long single. He, as a consequence, understands more than most the importance of caring and commitment in life. He would not wed except one who made forever seem too short a time."

"Then she is a fortunate bride and to be congratulated. But promises are broken."

"Looloo lived near falls, but I cannot remember the name."

"I could paint a bed with brightly coloured coverlet," Mrs. Pebbleship demonstrated the benefit of intense concentration. "An excellent choice, *bed*, because it has three of the early letters in the alphabet."

"Dog Falls!" the vicar pounced on the memory. "That was it!"

Mrs. Pebbleship assumed the vicar rejoiced with her artistic decision and continued. "I think we can move on to the *C*'s."

Rutland would ignore the elder couple's conversation to answer the sorrow in his elegant waif's voice. Hard to forget pain, he knew. Still easily recalled was his gut-wrenching disappointment on first viewing the charred remains of Gaunt's mansion. Though Rutland was familiar with war's devastation, he had never faced mindless destruction with complacency.

"No promises broken by this bridegroom, Mrs. Smith."

"How do you know?" The compassion in his eyes penetrated Lady Sarah's defences when fierceness had not.

"Because he has enough experience to appreciate the jewel he married. He has *dumped* past *disasters,* as has his bride, and both are ready for an eternity of *devotion, desires* fulfilled.

"There are your *D*'s, Mrs. Smith. And an *E* for good measure. Think of it, Mrs. Smith. An *eternity* to slake their desires." The wicked teasing returned to his voice and his eyes.

"Awesome to contemplate, Mr. Rutland."

"To contemplate, perhaps, Mrs. Smith. But to do, that is quite another matter," he growled as his eyes continued their examination of her yellow dress, plastered to very suitable curves.

Oh, that grin of his! What if she were to confront him, pull his head down, and bite that full lower lip? What if? She knew what he would do and laughed. Oh, to be the bride on Rutland's word card!

"*E* is for *Edward.*" Featherstone Smith's resonant voice unwittingly meandered into the conversation. "I do not believe I ever told you, Sarah, but Ned almost drowned near Dog Falls." The father smiled over the happy conclusion as he reminisced. "An intrepid little fellow. Always was. Well, he had done just what he was forbidden to do. Never gave up, though. Just kept thrashing about till he got close enough for me to reach out and grab him."

The cleric leaned forwards to address both Mrs. Pebbleship and Jack Rutland. "Do you know my Ned?"

Rutland had turned away in momentary exasperation to watch the water attack its many courses over the limestone. Always a lesson, watching water's eroding force.

He had not listened to Featherstone Smith's prating, but shook his head anyway at the parson's inconsequence.

Mrs. Pebbleship replied to the unheard question, hoping she had guessed the topic. "The words we teach must be relevant. *Cat* and *cow* come to mind." Deaf she was, but not blind, nor insensitive. Strong emotions crowding under the rock ledge would be better expressed when the two involved were alone. "Mr. Rutland, we cannot spend the whole of the afternoon under this rock when there are word cards to be made. Shall we go on? I think the rain is almost over."

"Never gives up, my Ned. Intrepid, I say." Featherstone Smith clutched his daughter-in-law's arm as they started up the path again. "I expect we will see him soon, eh, Sarah?"

From in back of them, assisting Mrs. Pebbleship, an implacable Jack Rutland returned to his alphabet. "Since we have a faithful groom bringing happiness to his bride, we need to consider the *I*'s."

"*I*? *I* is for *intrepid*," said the fond father of disobedient Ned.

In my alphabet, thought Lady Sarah, *A* is for *adultery*, *D* is for *dishonour* and *disgrace*. And *E* . . . is for *Edward*. Her destiny must lie in honouring their marriage vows.

As Mrs. Pebbleship traversed the old packhorse bridge and disappeared down the track leading to her son's farm, the clergyman sought to pursue *his* alphabet. "*K* is for . . ."

Kiss? The word immediately entered two minds. Neither reacted in any appropriate fashion, but Jack Rutland took every opportunity to help Lady Sarah along the path, flint striking steel each time they touched. Though the rain had stopped, Lady Sarah felt as if she were drowning.

"The Kingdom of Heaven! *K* is for The *Kingdom* of Heaven."

E is for *Edward*. *Edward*. *E* is for *Edward*. Like an incantation, she repeated her husband's name until she reached the safety of the kitchen's scarred table, where she could concentrate on making new word cards unimpeded by the chatter from Stable John's married sister. The comforting clunk of her spoon, the clang of iron pot would be promised respite, if not rational solutions for the sorely pressed gentlewoman.

"When you get to the *W*'s, Mrs. Smith, you might give thought to *weddings*." Rutland smiled his wry smile before he slipped from the kitchen.

He had shed his role as education's patron and was again the disciple of "Turnip" Townshend, Coke of Norfolk, and other heroes in agriculture. First the *C*'s. *Comb* and *cabbage*. Easier than drawing a cat or a cow, yet relevant for the mill women and children. Then she drew a door, half open. A welcoming door, though it did not seem to hang quite straight. Her technique with paintbrush ranked near her proficiency at embroidery.

"I like *D* for *day*, Sarah," her father-in-law advised. "A *dawning day*, with all its mellow colours." He sat by the hearth, softly singing his old song.

Rutland missed the evening meal. Alone in the kitchen, Lady Sarah completed a creditable dawn as she waited for him and decided to essay a ewe in the unlikely event the *E*'s would be reached tomorrow. Portraying a sheep was not too difficult, if one gave it a lot of fleece. Best to be prepared for every eventuality.

It grew late. Lady Sarah rubbed her eyes and the back of her neck. Rutland had not returned. She had been listening for him. Was he off courting? Planning a wedding, as in *W*?

He had been too familiar by the river. After all, they had never even been properly introduced!

This awful propensity of hers to find the ridiculous in the most serious of situations was perhaps her only talent, and hardly a ladylike one. Rutland must not think her so lost to virtue as her unconventional arrival might lead him to believe. She would remind him of her married state and the business relationship to which he had agreed. A laugh tinged with rue hid her chagrin. Married state, indeed! Nonetheless, she must do this as soon as possible.

Was it possible, for them to be friends and colleagues? Not when she could recall so vividly the gleam of his flesh through his wet shirt—the tingling file when he touched her. And she knew he looked on her with approbation, undeterred by a wedding ring.

Stars shone from a cloudless night sky as she walked across wet grass to the solar in the ancient manor house. Halfway up the outside stairsteps, she dropped down to lean against crumbling stones in the one side to the staircase and hunt for the North Star. There it was. Edward had enjoyed showing her the constellations in the sky. She did not speak, but watched his stride when Rutland appeared around the stable end of the manor house and mounted the incline to vanish through the ballroom doors. No sign of a lighted candle came from within.

It would not do, to enter that dark interior and tell him. What had she planned to tell him? Only with perfectly organised wits could she resist further involvement at Chance when he seemed able to rout her firmest resolve in their every dialogue.

=13=

IN SUCH HUMIDITY, even splashing sounds from the river's accelerated flow had no cooling effect on Lady Sarah as she hurried along its bank towards the mill. She had come to hate the confinement of hats, but would have welcomed a bonnet on this day. She paused to wipe moisture from brow and neck and shifted the burden of word cards, including Mrs. Pebbleship's giant tribute to canopied beds, collected on the way. The widow had elected to remain at home plying paintbrush to a sudden inspiration for the *F*'s, leaving Lady Sarah to deal with lessons and Bibby Bibbrow freed from Rutland's demanding presence.

Ahead, a line of alder trees separating meadow from mill yard shimmered in the glare of the sun. Their dappled shade offered an ideal location for the classroom today. She mounted the steps to the mill office and braced for confrontation with the ogre.

"Mr. Bibbrow! A hot summer day after yesterday's rain showers."

Too hearty a greeting, she knew, but hoped to counter his antipathy with great cordiality. It simply would not do to destroy Jack Rutland's careful negotiations. Bibby Bibbrow had been hunched over his desk and straightened at the well-tempered freshness invading the oven temperature of his cubicle. "So here she comes, ready to do good at my mill. Floating in like some snowflake, and lasting just about as long."

He chose to disregard the contradiction of her flushed cheeks, which added to her allure, feeding his resentment on the white muslin gown generously trimmed with eyelet embroidery and doubtless expensive.

Lady Sarah swallowed her consternation. Why such animosity? "A bully to the weak." She remembered Rutland's words. Did the master of the mill works employ civility only in Rutland's presence? She wished for that gentleman's cool assurance.

Her silence encouraged Bibby Bibbrow. "Trying to make people better 'n they've a right to be. Teach 'em to read, and the next thing they'll be disrespectful. Talking revolution. Like those damned Frenchies!"

He took a deep breath, necessary to fuel his anger in such suffocating heat.

Surely he did not expect those cowed women and children to turn on him once they learned to read, even if the stone mill must seem the Bastille of the Midlands. How would Rutland deal with this? Lady Sarah tried to imagine herself in his shoes—boots, rather—while taking note of yesterday's letter and word signs leaning against the wall in a neat row, as if the heat left them too weak to march against ignorance. What were they doing here on the office floor? Belle had wanted them on the walls of the dormitory upstairs.

Bibby Bibbrow in the meantime, having aired his recipe for revolution, sought to rid himself entirely of the cockoo in his nest. "A woman that reads is about as useful as a dancing dog." Above his grim little smile, pale eyes stared intently into Lady Sarah's. Was this the executioner's look as he swung the axe over Charles Stuart's neck? Lady Sarah clutched the newest teaching aids to her breast as a shield and turned again to the array of cards on the floor, placed where only Bibby Bibbrow could see them.

"And barely worth fustian," he finished the slur.

Why would he not allow the letters and the words up

in the dormitory? Where was the harm in having them there? Within the room's close limits, silence pressed as heavily as heat. Her clammy, perspiration-soaked shift stuck to Lady Sarah's body, adding to the discomfort. How should she answer this man?

"Taking profit away from an honest man what's worked hard for longer 'n you've been born." Fervour spent, he only grumbled.

Lady Sarah shook her head and stepped closer to the door, with glass window framing spinners and carders at their machines. Hiding behind a mask of composure, she appeared unmoved by the manufacturer's complaints, yet willing to listen to his entire inventory of grievances.

"End up in the poorhouse. That's where I'll be." The enduring silence had reduced him to sputtering. "Where will *you* be then, with all your fine clothes and fine airs? Not helping me, I can guess."

"But I would, I promise," said Lady Sarah solemnly, sensing suddenly that she had the advantage, but not knowing why. Like a clock, the ogre had wound down. "But I doubt you will be there," she hastened to add in response to a new storm rolling in over the creased forehead and hunched shoulders. "Instead, the role of benefactor might lead you—" She sputtered, too stunned at her ascendance to wield facile lie, "—to a line in the history books."

His chair squeaked in the sweltering cubicle as he read-justed his bulk. Narrowed eyes raked her face as he tried to determine if she was flouting his authority. Satisfied that she was not, he spoke in a reasonable manner, almost wheedling.

"Hardly seems worth coming out in the heat, to teach mill girls what spent all their lives at machines."

"But then *you* would not learn, Mr. Bibbrow."

"What do you mean?" Suspicions again flooded the pale eyes as he arose from his chair.

"I think you know."

She was groping in a game of blindman's buff, but an inability to read could explain his fears, not so unreasonable if he secretly shared the handicap of illiteracy. She needed to think on it.

"Have a care, Missus, baiting *me*. I read well enough to run this mill." He glowered.

"Of course. I meant we *all* learn during instruction, none more than the teachers. Now, we await your signal, for it is past time for the midday break."

She opened the door and flew into the clatter of machinery, the safety of numbers, before he advanced further on her person. He was not so menacing a figure standing in the gentle shadows of the alder trees, and his workers reacted accordingly. After soberly shuffling in close order across the mill yard, the group quickly developed new recruits who volunteered to identify *A*'s in the old words: *ark*, and *rain, teacher,* and *clean*—and the new ones: *bread*, and *bacon, cabbage, day*. Success begat success, and they sprinted through the *B*'s and *C*'s and *D*'s, ready and eager for the *E*'s. Thank fortune for the late night work on her fleecy ewe, thought Lady Sarah.

With the supply of word signs exhausted, an undaunted Lady Sarah found new ways to use the old. Vauncy Frome's dramatisation had not been lost on the former Queen Boadicea. She stuck the *A, B,* and *C* cards in the band of Belle's spotted teaching hat and bid her twirl slowly for the group to shout in unison as each letter appeared in front of it. Faster and faster, Belle spun round to the rhythmic chanting until all of the eighty could boast familiarity with the letters.

Lady Sarah's latent sense of fun, long buried in the formalities of her husband's hierarchical world, was fast becoming impossible to contain. Holding aloft Mrs. Pebbleship's version of *bed*, the elegant wife-reverting-to-hoyden sauntered around the perimeter of the group announcing, "*B* is for *bed*. *B* is for *bed*." Everyone joined in the new chant.

"What is this word?" asked Belle, holding up one of Lady Sarah's efforts.

The teacher's daughter was equally caught up in the uproar, and plunged back into teaching. Wat identified *C* for *comb*, and, imitating the beautiful lady, trotted behind her while students shouted, "*C* is for *comb*! *C* is for *comb*! *C* is for *comb*!"

Soon, every word sign was held high by a mill worker circling the others, shouting the alphabet. "*F* is for *Flora*," cheered that child, joining the parade with her letter card.

"*G* is for *Geordie*!" Belle armed another with his name letter and shoved him out into his peers' notice. Above limping gait, he proudly held his *G*.

"*H* is for *Hetty*!"

Gasping for breath, Lady Sarah halted off course to survey a spectacle of such vigour as should incite envy in the heart of the Fellow of the Royal Society. All that was lacking was Samson's chariot! She swayed from side to side in time with the marching tempo.

"*I* is for *Isaac*."

"*J* is for *Joan*."

How sweet was the excitement generated by learning! She must tell Rutland every detail! But it was past time to end the pageantry. Across the shaded area, she waved to Belle, who promptly herded her jubilant colleagues back to their machines. Lady Sarah gleaned from meadow ground the fallen cards and pictures.

Bibby Bibbrow, the only one untouched by it all, pronounced judgement from under the largest alder tree. "This is not the way to teach, Missus."

"Perhaps not, Mr. Bibbrow, but how stimulating! We may have invented a better way."

"Not for my millhands. I told Mr. Rutland I'd agree to let 'em learn to read the Bible. You bring the parson back tomorrow, to read something uplifting. A *short* story. Too much time taken today. More'n the agreement allowed."

Lady Sarah followed him into the stifling office. "Admit you were interested in our teaching today," she demanded of his broad back.

He sat down at his desk before answering. "I was. I admit. I like to see a dancing dog, too, every now 'n again."

No wonder Belle decried his smirk. Lady Sarah disliked it, too. He took such pleasure in toying with people, the smug toad.

"You can leave those things with me." he pointed at the cards and signs. "That bread and that beef look too pretty. I don't want anyone here getting ideas."

Not beef, but bacon. It was bacon. Was it his reading or her drawing?

"What about the letter cards? There is nothing tempting about plain letters. Pretty colours in the dormitory might encourage everyone . . . to work harder."

The master pondered. "Agreed." He jerked his head in assent.

"A line in the history books, Mr. Bibbrow." Lady Sarah bounded up the stairs to a dormitory floor even hotter than the lower one.

A battle won! Total victory resulted from numerous battles won, and in the end, the teachers would achieve total victory. If she had Edward's diamond-studded sword, she would brandish it—as he had done, at his banquet.

Lady Sarah darted to Belle's station and shouted in her ear above the noise. "The letter cards are lined up in the dormitory."

The drab spinster, worn dress stained with sweat, nodded comprehension.

"Next is better food."

Belle rolled her eyes.

"Yes!" Lady Sarah insisted.

Belle nodded as Bibby Bibbrow glared at the two from

Belle nodded as Bibby Bibbrow glared at the two from the door of his office.

Lady Sarah hurried from the room's implacable din. Across the yard, she never stopped until she reached the murmuring river, its waters sparkling in the sun.

So he wanted a few short uplifting minutes did he! How might the essence of his request be satisfied and still teach the ABC's?

Engrossed in solving the puzzle, she could shut out the discomfort of her trek up the steady incline in mid-afternoon heat. Much to do before tom—

"Rutland!" She had plowed into him and pulled back instantly. She would not have him feel her quickening heart beat. "I did not see you."

And a fine sight he was, in the simplicity of pale shirt and dark breeches, the comfort of worn leather boots. He was dressed for labour, but no one would mistake him for anything but master.

"How fares the teacher?"

"I wish you had been there today. Learning abounded." Open arms indicating the extent seemed more of a welcome for him.

"Tell me about it."

This was the way he liked to see her. Dauntless. Provocative in her animation. She seized his arm, as if wanting to increase the sharing, and over lively dialogue, they struggled up a steeper part of the path until Rutland called halt. "Mrs. Smith." Catching his breath, he took the time to admire every aspect of his companion. "You are more than meeting the terms of our business agreement. Happily, I can begin to meet mine."

He handed her the small pouch he carried. When she pulled open its drawstrings, she saw the gleam of her moonstone necklace. Strange, but she found more pleasure in his ready response to her request than in the return of the treasure. She shook her head at the contradiction.

"A carter I know—as close-mouthed as he ought to be—had a delivery to make at Madden and handily redeemed the piece."

Madden. Lady Sarah winced at the memory of disasters there but smiled into Rutland's watchful eyes. "You are a man to count on, Rutland."

His hand brushed from her temple a stray lock of hair and curled it around her ear. "Valuable jewellery, Sarah, for so small a debt."

"There was no alternative at the time."

"And how long must I guess at what troubles you?"

Grey eyes widened above the angelic white of her embroidered muslin. "Nothing troubles—" She could not lie, not under his steady gaze, and would not yield to the comfort, and more, she knew she would find in his . . . friendship.

She shrugged and twirled the pouch by its drawstring as she strolled towards shade ahead.

"As I recall, Sarah," Rutland recaptured her hand in the bend of his arm, "*C* is for *caring*, and I certainly care what happens to you."

"I care that Bibby Bibbrow plots to thwart us."

"I swear you teach him the art."

"No!"

"Then I have every confidence we will foil him . . . if his accounts show increased production at the end of the month."

"In the meantime, the man asks for nothing but short readings from the Bible."

"Patience, my friend. Though it may not seem so, we do advance."

"But how can our students learn if they are only read *to*?"

As they walked, passing under overhanging tree limbs, they disturbed patterns of sun and shade on the ground. Lady Sarah lifted her face to the coolness, inhaling an aroma different from that of the heat's blare. Rutland resisted the upturned face that wanted kissing to favour preserving their still tenuous relations and the touch of her hand tucked in his arm.

"I venture you have thought your way around Bibbrow's latest tactic."

"Yes. Though it will mean much work before instruction tomorrow."

"Curbing Bibbrow's high hand is tiring business I am learning. As constant as the turn of the mill wheel." Rutland wagged his head. "Food I sent for workers found its way to the village of Staples, where the tavern's improved meals gain in reputation."

"It will be more difficult for him now that you have me there daily."

"I keep thinking how fortunate I am to have a proper spy on my side. Apprehended with face already dyed for nights of reconnoitering," he teased. "I only wish I knew the circumstances leading to capture by our deputy constable."

"They are too preposterous for belief."

"Try me."

"You did say Bibbrow's lease expired soon?" She steered clear of rapids.

"One more year."

"One year, and then you achieve total harmony on your estate."

"No. For I find I like to acquire and revive lands others have mismanaged."

"And people, Rutland. You revive people."

"People like you?"

"Yes, and Belle. Stable John adores you."

"I would have that emotion surface elsewhere than in the stable boy."

"Do you find a teaching replacement for me?" Again, she skirted rough water. "You really search, I hope. It is July, now, and Father and I must go." She tugged on his arm.

"I am aware of the month." He continued to study the earnest figure, carrying a burden almost visible. "You enjoy the teaching?"

"Immensely. And being here at Chance as well. But I promised only a brief stay, while you spoke of every effort to find a teaching spy."

"Admit it is a difficult combination to unearth, particularly when one so perfectly suited to the task is already on duty."

Yesterday's rain had done nothing to disturb the river's indolence at the old packhorse bridge, which they crossed to follow the track to the Pebbleship farm.

"I count on Mrs. Pebbleship to produce a picture of a shepherd with his flock for use in class tomorrow."

"As in 'The Lord is my shepherd'?"

"Yes." Nice to have him perceive her direction. Nice to have his admiration, reviving her . . . like rain on the wilted rose she had been at Camford.

"Sarah. The Pebbleships beg you stay with them. Reluctantly, I have agreed."

"Leave the solar?" Lady Sarah attempted to alter her near wail into a guest's obliging tones. This sense of belonging at Chance was, after all, an illusion. "Father and I have intruded far too long, of course."

"Quite the contrary." He sighed. "A sad thing, yielding my designs on you to the Pebbleships."

"The perils of hospitality," she giggled. "But how kind."

"You can count on the Pebbleships."

"How kind of you," she explained to his raised eyebrows, "to politely relinquish your designs on me." And ensure proper chaperonage for a woman of quality.

He smiled at her understanding and pulled down vines blocking their way through the thicket straddling one of the river's tributary streams just past the bridge. "I believe your father will be content staying on with me and the stablehands." Rutland pushed aside more shrubbery. "He is close to completing his ravage of the old kitchen garden and should be allowed his triumph."

"Do you mind his ravaging of the kitchen garden?"

"Hardly. Old Mag might seek vengeance for the loss of her herbs."

Once clear of the thicket's spotty sunlight, they climbed towards the shelter offered by Rutland's major tenant in the house of grey stone that stretched its solid length between wooded ridges above and fields below. "A safe harbour ahead, Rutland."

He took both her hands and pressed them between his. "Sarah. The moment you want to leave, really want to leave, is the moment I escort you wherever you need to go. The ends of the earth sound appealing, if I travel in your company."

They laughed together at such foolishness, and Lady Sarah wondered why she must leave Jack Rutland's restorative kindness for the discomfort of Edward's contumely.

=14=

As soon as the red-nosed man had left, Aimée Orr, in linen and lace dishabille, streaked through the gilt-encrusted door to the salon that overlooked London's Grosvenor Square. An early morning sun of what promised to be a hot day gave further gloss to the decorations on Edward Bleddem Smith's uniform as he studied their alignment in the mirror, the top of which was guarded by a winged lion of gold. She sighed her satisfaction. How much more suitable a surrounding to display her hero than the hotel in Kings Street. This was not the time to be clutch-fisted—something Lady Sarah would never have understood.

"Well, *mon brave,* what did our ferret report? Is she at Long Wood yet?"

"No," he fulminated. "He can find no trace of her after Camford. Not at Long Wood, nor in Devon at her parents'." Britain's newest idol watched the blooming figure in the mirror and waited for her to reach his side, confident she would share his interest in correctly positioning the star of the Order of Saint Jonas. "Are you certain we can trust this fellow's discretion?"

"*Absolument.*" She had come a long way since her days as barmaid at the Dog and Duck, and nothing better illustrated the distance, she thought, than correct use of a few French phrases. "O.O. has known him for an *âge.*"

"Do you realise how it will reflect on my professional

competence if it is known that, though I can find and engage the enemy, I cannot vouch for my wife's whereabouts?" He turned away to pace the long squares of sunlight on the oriental carpet. "All the world and his wife wait for me to blunder."

"*Au contraire, mon brave.* The world and his wife want only to cheer you." Her hand on his arm halted the sunlit march. She began to stroke the back of his neck. "No one worries through the fracas, for this brave man'll not forsake us."

He nodded. "How many verses to your epic now?"

"Twenty-seven. I have had to stop for lack of rhymes with Napoleon and Bonaparte."

"Use Boney."

She disregarded the suggestion. Two weeks ago, Lady Sarah, with the reverend, had simply disappeared. Aimée had work to do, looking out for her future through her babe's interests.

"Come, sit beside me and feel your naughty son, who has been kicking me since you left our bed at dawn. Is it so terrible that you can't locate your wife when you have your Aimée?" Her finger followed his chin line and circled his mouth.

He relaxed against the saffron brocade of the sofa, its curved frame carved with bowknotted ribbons. "My wife," he scoffed. "Why would she do this to me, when her proper place is by my side? Doesn't she want to see me promoted, awarded honours, knighted?"

"Knighted? Others have won dukedoms. Why not you?" Aimée's enterprising finger smoothed the lines in his forehead.

"Because the jealous have always resented me, tried to discredit me. I suppose it is the plight of the extraordinary able."

Now her finger wound around his deep-set eyes and the prominent nose. Further details of his persecution were delivered less forcefully. "Recognition has been too long in coming, and, when it does, my wife deserts."

"Perhaps you could . . . divorce her. She *has* failed you."

"Divorce?" He reared in astonishment. "With the Corsican loose and my career on the rise?"

"And your son and heir born illegitimate." Aimée flounced into a pout at the other end of the sofa.

"Divorce is impossible." When Aimée would not comment, he continued. "Lady Sarah has been a good and loyal wife to me, as I have been husband to her. Only abusive cruelty or adultery could prompt a private act in Parliament. All quite expensive, and I could not marry again."

On hands and knees, Aimée swayed to his side and giggled in his ear. "She could be in some barnyard right now, with a new cock-a-doodle-doo. Have you thought of that?" She blew in his ear and collapsed, her head in his lap, and laughed at the unnatural idea of such elegance in a farmyard. "Of course, she would be a fool, to go elsewhere. When she had you." Aimée laid his hand on her swelling belly and pulled his head down to meet the invitation in her eyes. "But, then, *I* have you . . . So—"

Rising, she curled around his side and began toying with his medals. "Or, she might be lying dead someplace, killed by highwaymen and her body undiscovered."

Bleddem Smith squirmed in the silence that followed. "Highly unlikely."

Aimée persevered. "Your father might be dead, too. But he is old, and you could say it was time for him to go."

Bleddem Smith cleared his throat. "There have been no reports." His hand rubbed the crescent of her backside.

"It would solve the problem of your son's legitimacy."

"I will not hear any more of your ungodly musings, Aimée!"

"Probably why he kicks me all the time. Don't like the

idea of being born a bastard. Unable to inherit your dukedom."

He bolted the heat of her body for the window where a few faithful were gathering outside in the sunlight for a glimpse of Valhalla's anointed. He waved, as he took on the stern look expected of a man weighted with responsibility for defending the weak from the power-mad. Behind him, the door opened to admit the jovial Osmond Orr in dressing robe of a colour with the bottle he balanced with three glasses in his hands.

"An admirer of yours has sent over this excellent brandy, which I have sampled and pronounce worthy of your consideration. Both of you must try it."

Bleddem Smith impatiently refused. "Hardly the time for brandy."

"You have not tasted it. Aimée, I know you will join me."

"Guttling in the morning can only help me and my son."

"And in the afternoon?"

"The same thing!" Aimée whooped, and the Orrs raised their glasses to each other.

"Wait, my dear daughter. First we toast the bravest man in the world."

Aimée scrambled from the sofa, spilling some of the brandy on the saffron brocade. The pair's raised glasses aimed at Edward Bleddem Smith. "To the bravest man in the world. *Mon* brave *brave*" Aimée amended Osmond Orr's salute, and slumped against him, laughing helplessly at her use of both English and French pronunciations for the word.

"*Mon* brave *brave*," she repeated as, holding out the glass, she wriggled in advance on her hero. Osmond Orr's rumbling chortles encouraged her. "Guttle with me," she whispered as she fixed her body against Bleddem Smith and held the glass to his lips.

"The bravest man in the world deserves every pleasure

in the world," the sycophant boomed as he poured himself another glass of the fiery liquid. "And to our successful progress north. Before we finish, every citizen will have seen for himself the epitome of British heroism."

"What towns do we visit?" Bleddem Smith matched Aimée sip for sip from the glass of brandy.

"I believe you will want to avoid East Thorpe and Long Wood. Have to fob off questions there about Lady Sarah's direction," O.O. explained.

"I want to see Long Wood," Aimée objected. "Who has a better right to cheer the hero than his neighbours!" Her tongue momentarily replaced the brandy glass at Edward Bleddem Smith's lips. "Who's to know Lady Sarah ain't off in Devon?"

The master of Long Wood bobbed his head once in assent, but pushed away Aimée and her glass to pay closer attention to Orr and the progress arrangements.

"Then we go on to Long Wood from Ludbury." Orr confirmed the change in plans. "Take it in easy stages, considering Aimée, here. Shouldn't be from the city but seven or eight days."

"It must not interfere with sittings for my portrait. Aimée, you are seeing to it?"

"Would that Romney were still alive to paint you. To the portrait!" She had refilled her glass and was searching for things to toast. "Do you think this artist will do you justice?"

"He will, or we will find someone who does," the hero stated coldly.

"The Earl of Kettledene has extended a gracious invitation for a protracted stay. Longs to make your acquaintance," added Osmond Orr, master soother.

"Hmm." The hero seemed pleased.

"Your sister thinks she might have known the Countess when both were school girls together and hopes you will accept."

"Dear Emmaline." Aimée prepared for another toast.

"To your dear sister."

"Aimée," the factotum removed the brandy bottle from her hand, "will you be ready to leave within the hour? Our early departure this morning will go begging if we do not put the plan into action."

"She will," Bleddem Smith vowed.

"To Long Wood!" Aimée drained her glass and swept from the room, bumping into the door jamb as she did.

"A roving, a roving, a roving is my ru-i-in." The sound of shattered china accompanying her bawdy sea chantey deadened the fact that it was sung off key. No longer would a porcelain vase from the Ming dynasty adorn the mahogany table in the hall.

"My sister accompanies us?"

"Yes. As will your brother and his wife."

"A large party."

"Yes. When one achieves greatness, one can no longer travel light."

Bleddem Smith heaved a sigh, remembering past expeditions Sarah had led him on. Havey-cavey things, sometimes, but pleasurable.

"Inform the Earl of Kettledene we will be pleased to visit on our way back from Long Wood. One or two day's extension of our trip is possible."

Left alone in the salon, Bleddem Smith resumed the study of his medals as reflected in the gold-framed mirror. His fingers pressed against the neat rows. He would never forgive Sarah if she brought disgrace to their name, disgrace that would debase these medals. It had been a long, hard struggle to reach this point, and he deserved better than he was getting from her.

He had always been able to count on her. Why now, this sudden irresponsibility? Was ever a man so sorely pressed? He would find it difficult trusting her again. That is, if she and his father were still alive.

Did he care? She had been the stuff of dreams ten years ago. Though he had chafed at half-pay status, it had been lively to be with her. He never forgot he had married an earl's daughter. For most of their marriage, he had been gone, serving in the Indies, Egypt, and Holland. They had not been together enough, not enough, evidently, for her to conceive. Ha!

He backed up to get the full effect of his six feet in the mirror. Sarah had never given him an heir, and that mattered a great deal now. Actually, she had become a useless appendage to his life with Aimée, who was functioning as a woman should. If Sarah were indeed dead, his life would certainly be less complicated. He shook his head. He knew his earl's daughter did not have it in her to play the adulteress. At least he could always trust her there. His only hope lay in her death.

By God, if he wasn't an impressive-looking officer. He saluted the reflection in the mirror. The portraitist must reproduce the aura of command that surrounded him, had always surrounded him. Finally, everyone was seeing it too. Except Sarah. Damn her! If she ever disgraced him, made him the cuckold, he would destroy her . . . and the villain with whom she coupled.

=15=

"ALL OUR PICTURES are missing. Including the ewe," Belle Granger answered. She and Lady Sarah conferred on the day's teaching exercise as they led their band of scholars across the mill yard.

"Then after our lesson, I must ask him where they are." Lady Sarah straightened her shoulders at the thought of the interview.

"I'll go with you." Heartened by the aftereffects of yesterday's lesson, Belle allowed a bent for teaching to overset fears of her employer.

Lady Sarah shook her head. "Better if you stay clear of controversy. If he throws me out, you will be here to carry on."

"There!" Polly's soft voice was laced with excitement. "In the trees. See that *A*!" She pointed to a configuration within the line of alders. "Wherever I look, I see an *A*."

"I see it, Polly. How fast you learn."

Lady Sarah squeezed the young woman's hand to acknowledge her eye for letters. Wat tugged at the limp cambric in Lady Sarah's lemon yellow gown.

"There be an *H* in every window at the mill, and *B*'s in the front sign."

"Wat! You are reading!"

"All these letters 'round us, and I never noticed 'em afore."

Wanting to guard this momentous discovery, Polly glanced to the rear of the column where Bibby Bibbrow's scowl smouldered. He protected a black book in the crook of his arm.

Once by the trees, Belle handed to each millworker a small letter card to be matched to letters in the biblical quotation printed on a paper banner. Polly joined Lady Sarah in holding the span, the length of a man's spread arms, across which *The Lord is my shepherd, I shall not want*, wobbled in uneven but legible letters.

Reading the line repeatedly while Lady Sarah pointed to each word, Belle Granger imperceptibly ordered her flock. Given yesterday's success, the women and children needed little prodding. By threes and fours they came, carefully examining the interesting shapes of the letters before matching *E* for *E*, *H* for *H*, *L* for *L*. The younger and bolder, completing the assignment, called encouragement to the more hesitant.

The glow in Lady Sarah's heart reached her eyes. She had to blink, and blink again. Belle's teaching hat floated over a sea of proud faces—until the black figure of Bibby Bibbrow came charging through, a loose cannon aimed for destruction.

"I told you I wanted a reading from the *Bible*," He fired at Lady Sarah. Silence instantly settled over the buzzing group, schooled enough to recognise an end to happiness.

"This is from the *Bible*. One of the most uplifting quotations."

"You call this uplifting? Prancing up and down to match letters? Dancing dogs, I call it!" He swiped at the paper banner, tearing it from the two women's hands.

It sank slowly to the ground. The result of the entire Pebbleship clan's diligence until late last night—too late for their artist to paint a shepherd and flock—the crumpled banner lay inert. In the heat of midday, no breeze stirred the words of hope.

"You!" Bibby Bibbrow thrust his book in its limp black leather binding towards Belle. "Read from this. Every day, you just read from this."

He turned to an ashen-faced Lady Sarah. "This is what I want, and what I want is what we do at this mill, Missus." He paused to draw a deep breath. "You'd do well to remember it."

Bibbrow nodded at Belle, who began to read. "The Lord is my shepherd, I shall not want."

Still trembling over the cruelty of such senseless public attack, Lady Sarah reached out to clasp the cold hand of the quaking Polly.

"He leadeth me beside the still waters."

"Stand up straight," Lady Sarah whispered to the near-witless girl, and led her to stand beside Belle, where the three could be seen in support of dignity against a superior force.

"Surely goodness and mercy shall follow me all the days of my life."

Under the approving smirk of satisfaction that connected Bibby Bibbrow's jowls, Belle led a subdued line of students back to the mill and an afternoon's toil. Lady Sarah watched them shuffle past Polly's A-shaped trees.

A for *attack. B* for *bully. C* for *cruelty.* Alone in the sunny meadow, Lady Sarah collected their debris, along with her thoughts. She must ask about the pictures. Mrs. Pebbleship's canopied bed, the bread and the bacon, the ewe and the comb. The door half open.

Could Rutland salvage this? Lady Sarah remembered his counsel for patience. They did advance, slightly. There would be a daily reading.

And letter cards in the dormitory? She would make certain of that. With measured strides, she walked across the yard and upstairs to the pallet-crammed room, its low ceiling assisting the heat to stagnate. The cards were neatly stacked on one of the narrow beds. Now, for the whereabouts of the pictures.

"Mr. Bibbrow." She entered the lion's den. His dark brows threatening to collide above the bridge of his nose.

"Come, sir. It is too warm a day for the heat of anger." She stood quite still as he leaned back in his chair.

"Jack Rutland never said there'd be his fancy-dressed relative mixed up in the teaching."

"Fancy dressed? I merely wear my best to honour you and your establishment."

"Fancy dress and fancy talk don't belong in a mill, Missus. Now *there's* plain speaking." He rested his folded hands on the unbuttoned part of his waistcoat, which was spotted with stains.

Lady Sarah's eyes roamed all corners of the small office. "Where are the pictures we have used the past two days of teaching?"

"They're gone and not your concern."

"Gone where?"

"Just gone," His smirk indicated his enjoyment in knowing what she did not.

Lady Sarah looked away, knowing she could never win in a duel of evil stares, aware of a baking cubicle and a burning desire to destroy that superior smile.

"Gone to Staples, I suppose."

It simply slipped out, but she'd gained her objective. Bibby Bibbrow's complacency evolved into wide-eyed surprise.

"Will that do for plain speaking, Mr. Bibbrow?"

"I heard you were a spy," he hissed.

"An excellent one." She managed what she hoped was an enigmatic smile before turning her back, unsure of who had the advantage in the exchange of fire. Never before had she encountered such naked dishonesty. Through the window in his office door spread the dull blur of machines worked by people to whom he had granted less than she would have supposed, but more than they had had. She would act as if the advantage were hers and try for some harmony . . . for Jack Rutland.

"Mr. Rutland himself will, of course, discuss with you

the source of those tasty meals served in Staples' tavern. I presume Mrs. Pebbleship's paintings of bread and bed illustrate what is available there."

She stopped for breath. Eyes narrowed, Bibby Bibbrow glowered.

"How my poor depictions—bacon, a ewe, an open door—can be useful is past understanding, but how very agreeable if all were restored to the mill and fastened to the walls of the dormitory as soon as—tomorrow? Along with all the letters of the alphabet." She spoke in as firm a voice as she could muster, but low, as Rutland would do. "Then learning could take place so frequently, you would soon have the best workers anywhere."

Face now a protective blank, Bibby Bibbrow seemed relaxed in his chair, ready to agree to anything until free from the watchful eye of an outsider. Was he evil incarnate in Rutland's Eden, or only a poor, pitiful wretch?

"You must know of Mr. Rutland's success in restoring profits to his endeavours. Listen to him, Mr. Bibbrow, and find more money in honesty than ever you did dream." An impish glint surfaced in her eyes. "Do listen, and I promise never to return to your mill in any fashionably dressed capacity, spy or otherwise."

Bibby Bibbrow grunted. Lady Sarah extended her hand to him. "Agreed?" she coaxed.

"You made a mistake, Missus." He would not take her hand, but twitched his head back and forth as if there was little sense to what she said. He found it suddenly necessary to concentrate on the papers piled on his desk. "A sad mistake."

Lady Sarah forebore to contradict, not wanting to drive him to plot against accusations rather than ponder advice. Hand on the doorknob, she stopped for one final riposte. "For any small sum you care to offer, Mrs. Pebbleship would delight in painting countless pictures to exactly suit the Staples tavern."

Bibby Bibbrow pretended not to hear, riffling through

his papers. He opened a drawer of the desk to search its jumbled contents.

Lady Sarah left his office to rally dispirited workers, certain she did not offer false hope. "He needs persuading," she cried in Belle's ear, "but I think he is amenable. To our pictures on the dormitory walls, for instance."

Determination had returned to the deep green eyes, the set of the bony shoulders. Belle Granger had discovered the help that lay with well-placed friends. "We will prevail."

Lady Sarah stooped to cheer Wat, who scooted over the floor after stray scraps of wool that filled the box he dragged. "*B* is for *box*, and for *boy*," she pointed to his receptacle, then wriggled her finger on his chest.

"Polly, whenever you find a letter, stand very straight. It will help you remember." Polly complied as she called out all the letters found in her machine.

"You are learning to read, Rose. Flora, you are learning to read."

Lady Sarah's confidence grew as, heedless of the lowering presence in the office doorway, she walked the boundaries of the room's torrid clatter shouting assurance, willing them all to take heart.

Finally, she left, to tramp across the mill yard for the last time. The moment had come to leave Chance. She was no longer needed.

She must leave. The thought dictated the cadence of her steps back along the river path.

She could still help. Sending things from Long Wood. It would spur her to make an interesting life while she waited for Edward to resolve the tangle that trapped them. Edward . . . it was not his face, but Rutland's she saw. Rutland's strength and plans she had begun to share, and Rutland's raillery—implying an esteem and devotion she hungered for. She laughed, remembering his careful carelessness. He had restored her confidence in herself.

She must leave tomorrow, before deeper involvement with him erased all memory of her husband. Did Edward care, that she kept her word and remained true to their wedding vows, or was he too obsessed with Aimée?

That was easier to understand now, though the hurt stayed. He need not have flaunted the creature, expecting lies about her presence to conceal the dilemma.

More frankness would not have lessened the pain. However, in the lifetime that had passed since she left London, some of her anger had been tempered by insight.

Lady Sarah paused for breath. How tiring, to survive debacle at the mill only to cope with a steady incline, steeper today than it had been yesterday, surely.

No longer could she refuse the lure of the water. At the more secluded upper end of the Upper Falls, she left slippers and stockings on the bank near the ledge that had sheltered them all from the rain and waded into the shallow sweep of water. It poured over her where she lay, neck resting on limestone, her body floating free in the froth of a small pool carved from a level just inches below.

Was there a future for her with Edward and his Grand Design for rapid advancement until he was in command of . . . everything? Had she given him the help he wanted and needed? Not with influence, she hadn't. Her family's noble descent counted little in London's halls of power.

Had she inspired him to survive, to return safely from battle? Somewhere in Europe, was there a wife satisfied with her role as helpmate to the man who had killed the young lieutenant Davess, her brother?

A flickering pattern of sun and shade touched her eyes, and she had to blink several times. Life's patterns also fluttered in the slightest breeze, and nothing was ever the same again. Six—no, seven days ago, she had never heard of Jack Rutland.

"Jack." Tentatively Lady Sarah used his given name. "Jack," she called. The cascading water drowned the sound.

Reluctantly, she considered one last aspect of the Bleddem Smith marriage, an ache so tender she rarely touched it. No children bonded Sarah and Edward. She was a barren woman.

What did she care, showered with cooling bubbles of river water. She may have failed at marriage, but she had not done too badly with the alphabet lately. She smiled, remembering slate blue eyes that had assured safety and sympathy when she needed it.

"*J* is for *Jack*" she affirmed.

Jack Rutland, dismounting, led his horse into the heavily beamed interior of the great hall and the experienced hands of Stable John. Thirty acres with house and orchard now secured, the master of Chance craved planning a future to Sarah Smith's specifications and immediately headed down the river path to join her in the walk back from the mill.

He had existed too long without this woman who was so very special. He was as eager to embrace the traditions of married life with her as he was disinclined to partake of courtship's rituals. Let the wedding date be set by the time they returned. There was nothing to stand in their way.

Years of living on the outskirts of society were at an end for both of them. The younger son of a younger son of a disinherited line, he had never considered a career in the church. He was, as it happened, equally out of place among those who fought in answer to the demands of God, country, and His Majesty.

Well, Jack Rutland need never again take orders from fools, nor would his sons, if such should come to pass. In control of his life, he was free to make his own decisions, including the many that were less than astute. This decision—that Sarah Smith was the love of his life and must be pledged without delay—was so right and proper, it was like the decision to breathe. He really had no choice. Nor did he want one.

Engrossed in his musings, he stumbled over a familiar-looking pair of slippers, into which stockings had been neatly stuffed. At the same instant, he thought he heard his name penetrating the incessant babble at the Upper Falls.

His eyes scanned the wide stretch of river ahead, then back to where the falls began. There, almost indistinguishable from the foam, floated a yellow-garbed figure—his Sarah!

Without pausing to ponder the nature of her situation, he rushed headlong into the water, boots and all, plowing against the current. Fountains of spray splashed high with each step. Halfway to her, he lost his footing on the slippery, uneven terrain, so ill-suited for leather boots and fell to his hands and knees. "Sarah!"

She shot up, astounded. Her reverie! In the flesh! "Jack! Are you all right?"

She manoeuvred awkwardly to her hands and knees midst the swirling stream. Dripping and sputtering, they gazed at each other with wonderment, which quickly gave way to simultaneous laughter.

Still on hands and knees, Jack Rutland lumbered towards his Venus rising from the sea.

"Sarah!" he exploded. "My God, Sarah! Do you know how dear you are to me?"

He had not realised the depth of his wanting her with him for the rest of his life. On their knees, as inexorably as the water's flow, Jack and Sarah came together. Arms wound tightly around her, Rutland murmured endearments she did not hear, but felt in the closeness of their embrace.

Lady Sarah desired nothing more. Amidst surging waters, she responded to long-repressed emotions. Her wet arms clung to his wet, muscled back for the length of a heartbeat until, precariously positioned in the roiling water, they fell. Rutland tried to shield her as, still holding to each other, they tumbled with the current down a stairstep of ledges. Coming to rest in another shallow pool, they searched each other's eyes, and . . . memory returned to Lady Sarah. She rolled from the cradle of Rutland's arm onto her hands and knees.

"The moment has come, Jack Rutland," she gasped, "when I *really* must leave." She took a deep breath. "I am married."

She sat down, facing him, the water splashing her thighs. "I am married."

Rutland, believing himself guilty of frightening an innocent, had floundered to the other side of the shallow pool. Now, he threw his head back to gaze at the bright sky and inhaled deeply, to survive.

Married. She was married. What a wonderfully cruel joke. No winning turn of the cards here. No parson's daughter to be cherished, to bear their children. God! A married woman, true to her husband, and she would be. Oh, that her loyalty was his.

He had chosen to misinterpret the gold ring on the proper finger, and it was costing him dearly.

Rutland looked over at her, trying to get to her feet in the current's swirls and eddys. She closed her eyes when he moved to assist her. She kept them closed as he escorted her to the river bank.

"I should not have spoken," he said in a dead voice.

"Oh, please. No cold apology. I wish . . . I do not know what I wish. I wish I were still in your arms." Her grey eyes, open now, were filled with such pain, Rutland could no more refuse her aid and comfort than he could stop loving her. He drew her to him.

"I ran away from my husband."

Above the sound of the falls, Rutland could barely hear her voice muffled against his chest. "Tell me about it." He rubbed his chin across the top of her drenched hair. "Did he beat you? Abuse you?" he prompted.

"He abused my heart, my faith in his honour." She left

the solace of his arms. "I did not plan to run away. It just evolved as I stumbled from one folly to another on the way home."

"Like the nonsense over the blue face?"

"Yes!"

She retrieved her slippers and stockings. Rutland shed water-logged boots. They sat on a flat ledge, welcoming the warm sun.

"I never heard of such a nonsensical law." The veteran hostess restored order in the drawing-room.

"Men abroad at night with blackened faces are up to no good. Treason, smuggling. What was *your* reason for a blue face—aside from following ancient British custom?"

"I think it all came about through pure contrariness."

Lady Sarah tried to amuse him with her tale of travels with Vauncy Frome and Samson. When she donned her footwear, Rutland took some pleasure in sharing that small slice of domesticity.

"Then, we came to Chance, and you needed my help, wanted me to stay. It was what I needed and wanted. I could not leave."

Rutland arose. He gave her his hand to pull her erect. They would be better off walking if they were to talk of wanting. He carried his soggy boots as they plodded up the path in silence laden with words left unspoken.

But evasion was not for Rutland. "I have wanted you, Sarah, one way or another, since Derby W. Stout dragged you into my ballroom. And, one way or another, some day you will be my bride." He grinned his wry grin. "My *bedraggled bride,* as in *B.*"

"Never the wife for you, Jack. What would happen to your dream of sons and daughters inheriting vast holdings when I proved barren?" Lady Sarah kept her eyes on the trees ahead.

Jack Rutland halted their progress to hold her face in his two hands. "You, barren? As warm and loving and full of vigour and fun as you are?" Gently he shook her head. "Mark me. The day will come when you and I will prove the fallacy of this fear, Sarah. In the meantime, until your inadequate husband falls from his horse or overeats or succumbs to any of the ills flesh is heir to, you might continue on here, where your father can hone his skill with the scythe."

"My father-in-law."

"Ah . . . he can stay, too."

Lady Sarah grimaced at his try for denseness and shook her head. "I carry the hope my husband and I may eventually recapture part of what we had . . . once."

"And Ludbury is where the reconciliation comes to pass?"

"It is where Father and I connect with a coach to complete our journey."

"Your journey where? I would rather escort you to your final destination."

"No. I would not be at ease playing the stranger with you in front of people at Lo—home."

"I must accede to your wishes." He wanted no hint of scandal to taint her return, whatever that entailed. "First thing tomorrow, then, we shall go to Ludbury."

Such a simple matter, when he said it. "I worry when you agree with me so positively."

He cocked his head at her.

"Whenever you do so, I find myself involved in the exact opposite of what you agreed to."

He chuckled. "Would that be so bad?"

Now it was her turn to cast a questioning glance.

"You are right. I am not to be trusted too far. Sarah, are you certain you want to go back? You know how George the First treated his wife when she displeased him." God! This elegant waif needed watching over. He must learn her destination, her husband's identity.

"How?"

"Imprisoned her forever."

"This is the nineteenth century, and times have changed."

"The law can do cruel things to women. A man's property—"

"I do not want to hear. My husband is a civilised man of this century, and I promised, 'forsaking all others, so long as we both shall live.'"

"Yes." He must find time to query the father-in-law. He reached over and slid his finger down the nose of her earnest face. "Your husband *will* let you come do my books? Does he farm?"

"No."

"A merchant?"

"No."

"A tinker? A gypsy!"

"No." A warrior. Of tarnished honour. "How will you see us to Ludbury tomorrow?"

"I will exchange the future services of my ram for the loan of a very fine phaeton and pair of greys. I cannot have you and your father-in-law travelling any other way but first class."

"Particularly when we arrived under such *déclassé* circumstances."

"Exactly. See what a stay at Chance has done for you."

"Yes. I shall never forget it, Jack."

He would survive this, Rutland thought, as he had survived other blows. But, hellsfire, it was hard to face. This part of his dream had mattered the most.

"How did instruction go at the mill today? Was Bibbrow his usual cooperative self?"

"Oh, Jack, there is another problem."

They had so much to say to each other before they reached the old packhorse bridge and the parting of the ways.

=16=

"IF YOU HIRE a postchaise, you gain both privacy and speed."

Jack Rutland urged the choice on the Smiths as he tooled the double phaeton into the yard of The White Rose in Ludbury, bringing the vehicle to a stop by a side entrance whose porch supported thick rose vines competing with ivy for a place in the sun.

"But we are in no hurry," Lady Sarah assured him a little too brightly.

"I would rest easier knowing you were not at the mercy of some bosky coachman prone to drop you off in the middle of nowhere."

"Chance was not the middle of nowhere."

"Next time, you might not be so fortunate in your host."

Rutland, assisting her from the carriage, tried to play the stern guardian but was betrayed by his eyes, which devoured her. She stood there, enchanting him with her tucked silk bonnet and matching spencer the blue of forget-me-nots, an embroidered spray of the tiny blossoms almost hidden by a fold in the skirt of her paler-hued muslin gown. She was his own patch of blue sky to remember forever.

"Any more of your wandering must involve me." Rutland's wry smile accompanied the command.

"I cannot spend a shilling a mile in the hire, in addition to the generous tip one owes the postilion," she mumbled low as serving men converged on the equipage, "and I cannot take advantage of your offer of a loan . . . out of pity for your poor ram. An overworked beast, surely."

She took his arm as they followed the baggage into the coaching inn. Doubts over Edward's reception were gnawing at her, and she did not want to return home with a debt possibly subject to the scrutiny of Edward's fawning man of affairs—O.O.— the oily Osmond.

She could not, of course, accept an outright gift of money from Jack Rutland.

"You worry needlessly. The London coach is quite reliable, and in this fair weather must certainly come through on schedule later this afternoon."

That was brave talk, but little more. Trembling uncontrollably, Lady Sarah wondered if her legs could carry her any farther down the dark panelled hallway. Rutland's warm hand covered hers with the strength from his fingers. Her first sight of him, those fingers twisting the stem of his empty glass, welled through her. Then, she could go on after all, to engage a private parlour in which to await arrival of the coach that would put miles between them. It was left to the Reverend Mr. Featherstone Smith, still in the yard, to comment on the unusual stir of activity there.

"An extraordinary number of fine carriages here this afternoon," he said to the perspiring ostler. "That one," the cleric pointed to a large barouche, "is handsome enough for royalty."

"Aye. A signal day for Ludbury. We're having a hero's welcome. Tweaked the nose of Napoleon, he did, brave as you please."

"Indeed. Napoleon's nose. Remarkable. My son fights him, too, though I question whether he has seen the villain, much less hit his nose. He has never mentioned it."

"I'm sure he's a brave lad, nonetheless." The harried man trotted off, leading the pair of greys and phaeton that had, in five hours, sped the Smiths to Ludbury's only witness to fame since Richard of York rode through with his retinue and stopped to water the horses.

"Is there to be a party?" the vicar called after the ostler.

"A celebration at the Cloth Hall, since they don't spend the night."

Lady Sarah reappeared to retrieve her father-in-law from the inn yard's bustle. "I have ordered tea for us, Father."

"You know, Sarah, when I was a boy, I wanted to be a coachman. Sitting up there so high and mighty. In command of so much horsepower." He was reluctant to leave. "An exciting way of life!"

"Some might say you found a better way to serve the High and Mighty."

"Just as well. I was never easy imposing my will on horses. My Ned, he was the fearless one."

"Intrepid."

"Yes." The old gentleman beamed. "Has he come?"

"No. But soon, perhaps."

Was it her imagination, or had her father-in-law regressed during their mad journey? Perhaps he had been too long in the sun of Chance's kitchen garden. A sense . . . almost of forboding, hung over Lady Sarah. Intent on keeping apprehension at bay, she was impervious to the abounding air of excitement which the servants repressed in the interests of rendering faultless service, regardless of the occasion.

"Do you have our money, Sarah?" Featherstone Smith patted his pockets, "for I had none to give the ostler."

"I have just enough for us to reach Long Wood, if we are exceedingly miserly."

She had led him up the stairs to a lady's parlour midway down the hall. Through its open window, where a slight breeze teased the sheer curtains, could be heard the din of a crowd. As they both pressed for a look, blocked by intervening buildings, a cheer rang out, and another.

"There is celebrating at a Hall," the clergyman explained, moving to the plate of paper-thin cake slices that graced the Queen Anne table. "A local lad hit Napoleon."

"What!"

Seeing no reason for clarification, he munched on more cake as he observed the few pieces of furniture—the small settee and two chairs with cabriole legs grouped at the table, the whole set on a Turkey carpet as thin as the cake slices. By the tea tray, a vase of Bristol glass overflowed with white roses.

"Where is our coachman?"

"Mr. Rutland left to see to business."

"A nice fellow if there ever was one."

"You might tell him so when he returns."

Featherstone Smith swallowed the last of the cake slices as another cheer vaulted over the rooftops and echoed in the small room. The breeze from the open window beckoned.

"Sarah. I believe I will stroll over to see this brave lad. Fought in a mill with Napoleon and punched him in the nose. I wish I had seen it."

She wondered where the truth lay in his tale and knew he would not be dissuaded. She could leave a message, should Jack return before they did. The country town was not too populous.

"I will accompany you."

A square's walk and they stood at the edge of a scattered crowd of about one hundred citizens, grown bored with the extended formalities staged behind a stone balustrade that enclosed the Cloth Hall balcony. A flash of jewels from a sword flourished in the sunlight, and Lady Sarah knew at once who was being celebrated. Her heart raced as fast as her thoughts.

Edward had followed her! She felt her cheeks glow with relief. Why had he come? Oh, it did not matter. He had come. There was still a chance for them, for happiness.

"Do look." Lady Sarah overheard a goodwife croon. "I believe his wife is breeding. There'll be a little one before long to carry on the tradition of courage."

Aimée Orr, holding a pose of adoration next to the hero, rivalled his jewelled sword for sparkle. Metallic threads woven in the white fabric of her gown, false diamonds—they had to be false, there were so many—at her wrist and on the ribbons of the straw bonnet crowning the dark auburn curls, all contributed to her glistening presence in the bright light of early afternoon.

The carnival had come to town, thought Lady Sarah, and Aimée Orr is the tent. She lacked only a pennant. And there, as supporting players, were G. Featherstone and his wife. Where, pray, was widowed Emmaline?

The crowd hushed as Edward discharged his wintry monotone over the warm air. "All I ask is to serve my king and my country with honour."

"Sarah! Ned's come!" Featherstone Smith acted immediately on his discovery. He began to make his way, at an angle across a corner of the crowd, towards the dignitary-filled balcony. "Ned! Over here!" He waved his arm to catch his son's attention. "Ned! Over here!"

Edward Bleddem Smith lowered his ceremonial sword to note the disturbing sound. At sight of his father with Sarah behind, the hero turned his head briefly to speak in the ear of Osmond Orr, who in turn moved aside for words with a weasel of a man possessing a severely reddened nose, a reminder of January's cold air in July. The pair raised eyes to the advancing Smiths before the dark-suited weasel slipped inside the Hall from the balcony. Osmond Orr puffed down the outside staircase.

In that instant, the Bleddem Smith marriage dissolved. Lady Sarah, astounded by the lack of any sort of welcoming smile—a surprised one, at the very least, if not one of joy—ceased to follow in her father-in-law's wake. The whispered conferences on the balcony terrified her, as did the obdurate air emanating from her husband. She could feel the frost from where she stood, thirty feet away, as if he had given the order to take no prisoners. What might a husband do, in the nineteenth century,if he was displeased with his wife?

As her father-in-law drew ever closer to the balcony and his son, Lady Sarah hesitated before abandoning responsibility for his well-being. One more moment, and she turned to head in the opposite direction. Hurrying through the crowd, she scuttled from the town square as fast as was possible without drawing attention to herself.

First, she must recover the moonstone necklace from her trunk in the private parlour at The White Rose. It would translate to money in the event she did not connect with Jack Rutland and needed to pay someone to take her back to Chance. She gained the inn, the stairs, the dark privacy of the landing before finishing the climb to the first floor. She was gasping for breath.

"Lady Sarah!"

"Emmaline!" Lady Sarah halted, nonplussed. "How well you look."

Centuries of a tradition in courtesy prompted the genteel salute to her lavender-clad sister-in-law, but an even longer-established instinct for self-preservation propelled her on up the stairs after only seconds given to convention's demands. Emmaline, her brother's face a study in uncertainty, turned to observe the headlong climb.

"Do you join us at the Cloth Hall?"

Lady Sarah stopped at the top of the stairs. "Of course. But I am late, and you know how Edward feels about that. I beg you do not wait for me."

Her answer satisfied Emmaline who continued her descent, muttering about Edward's well-known, and totally unreasonable, insistence on promptness.

Shaken, Lady Sarah reached the door to the private parlour. Oh, let Jack Rutland be sitting there, on the other side of the door!

The empty room was strangely quiet. No crowd noises interfered with the refuge offered within. Did the endless speeches continue for an awe-struck crowd, or had the celebration come to a close?

The key! Where was the key to the trunk! She was all thumbs. Stop, and take a deep breath, she urged herself. Take two deep breaths. Lady Sarah stripped off her gloves. There was the key.

She struggled with the lock before the trunk would open. Removing the moonstones from the leather despatch case, she dropped them in her reticule and let the trunk lid fall. The thump was loud, and final.

Cautiously, she opened the door to survey the hall. Empty. All she had to do was find where the greys and phaeton were stabled and stay concealed close by until Jack came. Surely, such a simple plan was possible.

She mustered her last ounce of poise to glide back down the hall. The stable yard and some measure of safety were not that far away. Then, she heard Osmond Orr's affable voice resounding up the stairwell.

"A lady dressed in blue. Saucy hat, certainly. Mrs. Smith? I believe she stops here."

There must be a back stairs! Lady Sarah scampered to the far end of the hall and around the corner. Nothing but closed doors stretched ahead of her. An open window at the end of the ell offered the only egress.

She had no choice. She might have faced Edward, but she refused to deal with Osmond Orr. Never would she forgive her husband for sending that churl after her.

She managed the climb out of the window, but the steep pitch to the roof prevented any reconnoitering. Clutching at the ivy-covered walls, she inched her way to stand just past the open window, out of view of anyone in the hallway.

From this position, with her back to the wall, she could claim a view—somewhat impaired—of the stable yard to her right, through the rustling leaves of a large oak tree.

In its shade, and reassured by the summer breeze and the scent of roses from vines climbing towards her up the slope of the roof, Lady Sarah prepared to wait until she could spy Jack Rutland or a Smith party exodus . . . or until hell froze.

=17=

HE WOULD GIVE the money to the parson on the sly, thought Jack Rutland as he left the bank. Tell the poor soul it was Smith money. That would give them adequate funds for wherever they were going, with Sarah none the wiser, until it was too late. From what little she had let slip, he had an idea of events prior to their Chance arrival, and he wanted no more smokey situations plaguing their travels.

Approaching the square, he asked of a townsman, "Whom do we celebrate?"

"Bleddem Smith, victor against the Corsican adventurer."

"I have heard of him." And his reputation for glory seeking. Rutland gazed across the square's expanse to the be-medaled centre of all attention. Brave, to give the man his due . . . when it suited.

The former warrior sought to by-pass all the commotion for the most expeditious route to The White Rose. He needed to put in motion his financial aid plan before the coach pulled in. In truth, he needed to waylay the coach, that was what he really needed to do. He could not believe he was letting this woman go out of his life without putting up some kind of fight. God! He was getting old. Just a step from Featherstone Smith's addled state.

And Bled 'Em Ned won the crowd, Rutland mused. Edward Bleddem Smith, hitting a thousand scattered

throngs in a thousand different villages, until he entered
Parliament—if he survived hostilities—and bored it to
death, bringing an end to civilised government as
Englishmen knew it.

Rutland entered The White Rose through the same
side door he had used on his way to the bank and almost
stumbled with the impact of the words remembered. " '*E*
is for *Edward*,' the little parson had shouted out at the
Upper Falls. 'Do you know my Ned?' Was his son the six
feet of heroism there in the town square?

Perhaps, Smith was an assumed name. No. Rutland
discarded that notion. The parson did not have enough
wit remaining to carry it off. Let's see, Edward Bleddem
Smith was married to an earl's daughter. Lady . . . something.

With deliberate speed, Rutland mounted the stairs.
Lady Sarah? Was that the name of Bleddem Smith's wife?
His Sarah? Had she already returned to the top-lofty hero
in the vain hope of finding happiness listening to his
public speeches down through the years? Not *his* Sarah.
She would not stand for it. And they had not said their
last good-bye.

Ahead of him, a burly gentleman knocked and opened
the door to the private parlour Sarah had engaged. Rutland withdrew, down the stairs. Nothing must mar her
reputation. He could imagine what scandalmongers
would make of their few secluded days at Chance. He
withdrew, but he would not leave until he knew all was
well with her. Rutland headed for the stable yard to learn
what the ostler knew.

"Well, I tell you," said the ostler scratching his head.
"The lady you're enquiring about is up there on the roof."
He bobbed his head in the direction of the large oak tree,
standing sentinel at the other end of the yard. "Happened
to see her come out a short while ago."

Rutland looked in the direction indicated.

"You can see her through the leaves. Don't know

whether she's admiring the view or what." The man was obviously puzzled.

"Ah, yes." Rutland caught a glimpse of blue behind the bank of roses on the roof. If she were Bleddem Smith's wife no wonder she was on the roof. "I think you had best hitch the greys to my phaeton, ready for an immediate departure."

He spoke nonchalantly, and tipped the man well, though not overly so. The less memorable the incident, the less likely the ostler would long recall it.

"It'll be done, sir."

"She gets these spells, you know."

"Frail creatures, all right, women."

Back into The White Rose, and up the stairs, Rutland started down the hall as the burly man stood in the open doorway of Lady Sarah's private parlour. In one over-sized hand, he held a pair of white kid gloves.

"Have you by any chance seen a young woman in blue. Wears a particularly fetching blue bonnet." He chuckled. "I worry about her when she's late."

Rutland managed to look askance at the familiarity. "My good man." He shook his head as he continued on down the corridor and around the corner to the open window.

He sat on the sill, facing the corridor, where he could see anyone approach. "Sarah. It's Jack." He spoke softly, so as not to startle her, and backed his arm out the window to reach where he knew she stood.

"Jack!"

Her soft hand was instantly in his. He held it tightly.

"Oh, Jack!" She was so grateful to have him here! She had begun to feel ridiculous, out on the roof. "I want to get away." She spoke in his conspiratorial tone of voice.

"From Bleddem Smith?"

"His minions."

"I met one coming out of your parlour. Are there more?"

"One with rosy cheeks, as if someone smacked him in the face with a paintbrush."

"And that's all?"

"I do not know. I have been busy hunting back stairs."

"Shh." Rutland folded his arms across his chest and disdained the curious stares of a portly gentleman leaving his room. When he had disappeared around the corner, Rutland tested the nearest door, with success.

Returning to the window, he put his hand out to Lady Sarah and slowly pulled her towards him. "I found the stairs."

He lifted her across the sill and opened the correct door to a back stairs, haunted by a musty odour. Still holding her hand, he led her into its dark confines.

"How did you know where to find me?" she whispered.

"Later. I presume your father-in-law does not join us."

"He is safe, with his children."

"Who was the large and amiable man guarding your sitting-room?"

"Osmond Orr."

"He has taken quite a fancy to your blue attire. Especially the hat. I venture everyone will soon be looking for a woman in blue."

At the foot of the stairs, Rutland eased open the door a crack, and, as quietly closed it, motioning Lady Sarah to back up. Where the stairs curved, he pulled at her to stop. "Your rosy-nosed friend makes himself at home in the kitchen, where he has a fine view of the door we must use." He spoke softly, next to her ear.

Lady Sarah, standing on the step above him, dropped her head to his shoulder. His hand stroked the nape of her neck, moist with perspiration, and brushed up against the twisted knot of her hair.

"Whatever happens, Jack Rutland, I want you to know—"

"What is going to happen, sweetling, is your transformation. How, is the only problem."

"Hmm." She raised her head. "Yes!"

He sensed her sudden rise in spirits, her slim body pulsating with it. She pulled from her head the blue tucked silk confection and stuffed it in her reticule. Releasing her hair from its knot, she shook its soft luxuriance, the clean smell inviting his hands to feel the texture.

His loving gesture was stopped by her whispered command. "Take off your coat and shirt." She began to assist him as he awkwardly manoeuvred within the narrow space and pretended grumbling compliance.

"This is neither the time nor the place for love making, sweetling."

"Yet you prepare." Impossible to resist his insouciance. She lost all dread when she was with him.

"I am an obliging fellow. And it *is* cooler this way."

She donned his white shirt as she explained. "They look for a woman in blue hat and dress. Therefore, I shall become a woman clad in white."

"Excellent. And of course, a half-naked man will draw no attention at all," Rutland retorted softly. With her help he slipped arms back into coat sleeves, and struggled attempting to tie his cravat.

Lady Sarah took over the task, working on a bouffant design to hide his sartorial limitations. "There! No one will notice you have no shirt." She admired her quick handiwork in the gloom.

"Is this tied in a Mathematical?" he enquired of her design.

"No. A Sarah. The very latest. Puts you in the first stare of fashion."

"Our success is assured—if you play the tart, and I, the April-mad beau."

"Agreed." Shivering, she pressed her cheek against his. His hand caught her chin and held it as his lips moved across hers. "Let us begin our little drama."

Opening the door against the to-do in the kitchen, Rutland swept Lady Sarah into his arms. His long legs could best disguise swift passage, while a Lady Sarah over his chest further ensured against anyone noticing the absence of a shirt. She kept her face dipped in the puffs of his cravat and giggled during the entire progress through cloud of steam and drift of downy feathers where a maid plucked chickens. Rutland ducked to avoid pots dangling from an overhead rack and sidestepped the twitching tail of a tabby intent on the swish from the butter churn.

Snuffling rhythmically, the weaselly Red Nose gave the intruders one rheumy eye. the other was fixed on the flour-spattered hands of a matron who deftly manipulated dough destined for water-specked cherries, twinkling like ruby stars after their rinse in the sink.

Only a child chipping away at a block of sugar really observed the couple, soon gone from out the cerulean blue walls, the very colour known to keep flies away. The White Rose strove to stay up to date in every service area.

True to his word, the ostler had the phaeton ready. He frowned. "What did you do about your friend on the roof?"

"I delivered her to her father," answered Rutland, highly pleased the stable man saw no connexion between the woman on the roof and the one in the carriage.

Lady Sarah giggled once more for good measure from behind a coy glance as Rutland tossed the fellow a final silver coin. They were off, the greys soon executing a brisk trot.

"Is this the right way to Chance?" asked Lady Sarah in alarm.

"It is if we want to leave a track impossible to follow."

"Why do we want to do that?" Lady Sarah chafed, suddenly drained of all vigour and longing for the relief from the strain of the last hour.

Rutland did not take his eyes from the horses, from the road. "We are fleeing Bleddem Smith, are we not?"

"Yes."

"Then we do not leave him any invitations to join us

at Chance."

"Why would he want to come, when he has lost interest in me?"

"Because, sweetling, he has a reputation for unswerving devotion to destroying the enemy, and you might well have become one now."

"How can I be his enemy? I am his wife!"

"Not when he sends two ruffians after you."

To think the day had come when her husband, her loving husband of the moonstones and watching stars and so many intimacies had become her enemy. "What . . . what happened to our marriage?" A keening wrenched from her soul. The outcry disappeared in the sound of the horses' gait.

Rutland let her weep. The death of dreams was as difficult to bear as any other death.

"I am sorry," Lady Sarah murmured when she had regained control. "This has been a . . . a rather unusual two weeks."

"And you are not through yet. Time for a costume change."

He turned off the main road, towards seclusion in a nearby copse. Lady Sarah returned his shirt, and, pursuant to his instructions, restored the blue tucked silk atop brown hair worn once again in its classic knot. A woman smartly attired and bonnetted in blue, she would have roused envious stares in Hyde Park at five of an afternoon, but for the droop in her shoulders and the chalky hue to her complexion.

"Are you a horsewoman, Sarah?"

She shook her head. "No, but I can do what is needed." She straightened her shoulders and managed a smile which was a little more lopsided than usual.

Rutland studied her. He had wanted her to drive alone through the hamlet ahead, turning off at the first available wooded lane where they could have rendezvoused. Given her spent condition, it was better to sacrifice this part of the plan rather than risk the whole. He folded his blue coat and laid it on the seat of the phaeton as cushion. At least, in shirtsleeves, he could be taken for a hired servant rather than a loving accomplice.

"Should the occasion arise, I want the citizens of the village ahead," he pointed towards the main road and a church steeple in the distance, "to attest to seeing a woman in blue travelling through in a northerly direction this afternoon."

Had her father-in-law called? Lady Sarah's eyes opened to pitch black. Where on earth was she? Then, she remembered.

"Rutland?" she whispered tentatively, squirming to improve the comfort of her position against the tree trunk.

"Still here."

"I believe I fell asleep for a few minutes." As her eyes adjusted to the dark, she could discern part of his outline against a tree across from her in the small glade. Just beyond, the horses cropped the grass contentedly.

"Do you think our strategy has succeeded?"

"Time will tell."

"That is not the answer I wanted. I doubt there is a country lane we have missed on this circuitous route to Chance."

His laughter was low in his throat. "Maybe one or two."

"How wily you are." Her admiration warmed him in the little dell.

"Faint-hearted is more to the point. I did not like the size of the amiable pugilist in your husband's employ."

"I understand your fears. Osmond Orr could toady you to death."

"Never underestimate the opponent, Lady Sarah." Rutland did not banter now.

She matched his mood change and his quiet voice. "I know you risk too much in helping me."

"Society does not award medals for spiriting away another man's wife." Once again a teasing tone underlay his words.

"I owe you . . . my happiness."

"Are you happy now?"

"In this haven? Yes. Are there medals for kindness and making the worst of times seem almost pleasurable in your company?"

"The Order of Bacchus. Cooing doves rampant on a field of wild oats."

"You see." she looked about her. "This is an enchanted place where nothing can harm us."

"Indeed, Lady Sarah."

He would not mention stray livestock, vermin, beggars, tinkers, and . . . scandal. He had, at least, eliminated Bleddem Smith forces, if only temporarily.

She rose, fully awake now, and started towards him, longing to banish the formality of "Lady Sarah" on this midsummer night, needing to feel solid reassurance.

"No you don't. You stick to your tree, and I'll stick to mine. Those are the rules tonight, Lady Sarah. I will not have you drowning in a divorce scandal, an outcast suffering cuts from those not fit to wipe your boots." He spat out his fears for her, passion mounting over mean years before the landmark card game. "When we marry, my lady, it will be done amidst loving best wishes from all quarters. My family's line has had enough of being the object of whispers. I do not want it for you or our children."

"When we marry," Lady Sarah repeated softly, unbelieving and unwilling to fantasise.

"It will happen. Time is on our side."

"What do you mean?"

"I mean your hero husband will chase after glory one too many times."

"I cannot wish for that."

"I know. But it will happen."

"And when love turns to hate?"

"Ours will not, my lady."

"Why would it be different?"

"Because we will guard against it."

A lullaby of night noises promised peace. The small brook babbled of Arcadia. There was time for Lady Sarah to realise the enormity of Jack Rutland's willingness to sacrifice all he had won and worked for—just to help her. She must not allow it—scandal, staining the rest of his life with whispered slander. She moaned. Surely, Edward would not demand satisfaction. It did not bear thinking so.

If she found a farmer in the neighbourhood, a countryman less suspicious of the unusual than that idiot constable—if she found a farmer of Mr. Pebbleship's ilk with a cart, she had the means to reward him for transportation to Long Wood. Armed with the moonstones in her reticule, she could save Jack Rutland.

"Jack."

There was no answer. She thought she detected the steady breathing of sound sleep.

"Jack."

It was now or never. She could regret later not saying good-bye. With cautious steps, she slipped from the small clearing. Which way lay the road they had left? Reviewing in her mind the twists and turns of their journey, she tried to remember the last farmhouse they dodged.

There! The North Star. A friend in need. She eased though underbrush, but tripped in the darkness on the twisted root of a tree and fell, against Jack Rutland's warmth.

His strong fingers gripped her shoulders. "Is it modesty that drives you so far from our camp?"

"No."

"Then please do not do this again."

"Help me to free you—from me. The accompanying hazards threaten your future."

"The future I want is worth the gamble, Sarah." He backed away from her. "One minimises risk by exercising all necessary precautions—which we have been doing." He extended his hand. "If we would reach Chance before dawn, we should leave now."

Her slender fingers gripped his, shifting until both man and woman found a satisfying set to the clasp. Perhaps circumspection was their best weapon, thought Sarah, and her presence a pledge against mayhem.

"I gave thought to my decision to leave the glade," she explained.

"A testimonial I shall treasure, later." He lifted her onto the carriage seat. "I should not have spoken as I did, destroying your enchantment with this place."

Once more on a road more readily recognisable as such, Lady Sarah broke through the mesmerising rhythm of the trotting horses. "Jack. Was I heading in the right direction, in my bid to win your freedom from this morass?"

"High marks for navigation, my lady. However, as far as I was concerned, you were heading in the wrong direction."

=18=

"I TOLD YOU, Ned. Sarah and I were at Dog Falls." Featherstone Smith had a sudden flash of recall. "By Chance."

"Your entire escapade was a chance thing, Father, and not what one of your age and dignity should have indulged in, I vow."

"Do you remember, you almost drowned at Dog Falls?" The cleric turned to his daughter. "Looloo? You remember."

"That is your daughter, Father. Emmaline." Thwarted in these interviews by his father's incoherence, the war hero snapped out his curt reminders.

"Oh. Yes."

"What Lady Sarah was thinking of, I cannot imagine." Emmaline Nimble (née Smith) carefully counted threads before piercing the fabric with her needle. "Dragging Father away from London just when all his family gathered."

"And what were *you* thinking of, Emmaline? Not to have stopped her when you had the opportunity is equally bewildering." Edward Bleddem Smith turned on his sister. His inclination to attack was better developed than his skill in the interrogation of prisoners.

"She said she would join us."

"And you believed her?"

"Why would I not?" Mrs. Nimble stabbed the cloth, tautly pulled in her tambour. She embroidered violets of the same pale colour as her dress.

"Children! Do stop your quarrelling!" came a querulous echo from the past.

Flushing, Emmaline rested the tambour in her lap to watch her brother bring to life the ferocity of the winged beast that bared its fangs atop the mirror's gold frame. Back and forth and back and forth, the nation's current hero paced a path provided by the design on the carpet's burgundy background.

"I know you are vexed, Edward, dear, but I do not see how Lady Sarah's defection detracts from your fame. Do sit down, before you wear holes in the carpet."

He ignored her. "We have enquired all the way from Ludbury, north to Thorsgate and Dog Falls, and even on to Penfield. There is no trace of her."

"You almost drowned at Dog Falls, Ned. Do you remember?"

Via the mirror, the son exchanged a look of martyrdom with his sister. "There is no trace of her after she was seen travelling through Saint Kenelm in the phaeton pulled by two white horses—"

"You were intrepid, Ned. Kept thrashing about till I could reach you."

"Two white horses or a pair of greys, depending on which of the several witnesses you query.'

"Are you certain it was Dog Falls where they visited?" ventured Emmaline.

"That is the only thing Father keeps repeating with any surety."

"The wedding. What about the wedding?"

"Ah, yes. The wedding. With a Roman soldier. You would have us waste time by crediting one of Father's wildest fancies?"

"Where did you say you performed the wedding ceremony, Father?" Though inheriting her father's slight stature, Emmaline had her mother's tenacity, as well as Saxon colouring.

"Near the fountain. Not many attended since it was at night."

Vindicated, Bleddem Smith continued his martyr's role. "Why does Sarah embarrass me like this? Playing cat and mouse just when widespread recognition and acclaim are within my grasp and we must prove ourselves above reproach." He halted at a window and peered from behind the gold velvet drapery to the sunsplashed square outside.

Emmaline took up her embroidery again. "Remember Judas, and what the Bible tells us about people more interested in betrayal than in love. You are far too trusting, Edward." Skillfully, she plied her needle in the delicate floral pattern as she continued a family tradition of cosseting its own Sun King.

Aimée Orr burst into the gilt salon, waving a crested note. "The Earl of Kettledene has asked us back!" She kissed the air in Bleddem Smith's direction but approached Emmaline in order to admire the embroidery of a potential ally. Bending over the widow's chair, she interrupted the painstaking count of threads.

"A pity his wife is dead, Emmaline. Oh!" Aimée's face indicated the onslaught of inspiration, which she shared. "Do you suppose the earl has developed a *tendre* for our Emmaline? Is that why we are asked to return?"

She snatched at the lace cap topping Emmaline's bubble of fading blonde curls. "Time to forget your widow's garb and dress for flirtation, Emmaline. Who better to choose for a second wife than the first wife's bosom-bow, eh?"

Emmaline's cheeks reddened. " Do you think so? I thought that Mrs. Peake . . . "

"The housekeeper? Never!"

"And his dead wife . . . not who I thought she was. From the stage, I believe." Emmaline Nimble patted her coiffure, an aberration of the Titus style, in the belief she brought order to the disarray Aimée's playfulness had wrought.

"I question the propriety of attending a house party without a hostess, Aimée."

"You are too provincial, Emmaline."

"Perhaps." She shifted, uncomfortable in her chair, and looked over to her clergyman father.

"I could not like that big house. A cavernous pile. Had to sleep in the kitchen."

No one bothered to correct the old gentleman. He had *not* slept in the kitchen during their stay with the earl.

Aimée lounged on the sofa. "Do let us go again, *mon brave*. Soon. Such jolly times we have, guttling and gambolling at an earl's seat."

The hefty mistress affected a kittenish pout to lure a consenting nod from Bleddem Smith.

He, too, enjoyed the intimacy with a wealthy noble house, however recent the line. Kettledene collected noteworthy things, like a jewelled snuff box used by poor Frederick, deceased father of George III, and a gold toothpick once belonging to the Duke of Marlborough. Bleddem Smith pondered over which of his gem-studded decorations he would will to the earl. The Order of Saint Jonas?

"Where is Sarah?" Featherstone Smith struggled out of his chair and looked to each of the room's occupants, as if hoping one of them would bear the familiar face of his daughter-in-law.

"That is what we are trying to determine, Father."

"Well, why don't you go where she is?" Exasperation clouded the bland face.

"Where?" chorused the trio, hoping for a break in the fog.

"At Long Wood, of course. If I leave immediately, I can catch the first coach north." He headed for the door.

"There is none leaving in the afternoon, Father." Bleddem Smith inclined his head, delegating to his sister the task of handling the sad relic. "You will have to wait until morning."

"At least delay until after tea." Emmaline caught up with her father's retreating figure. "Something to eat, and he might not be so addled," she explained to the others as she led him from the room.

"And where is Osmond Orr this afternoon," Bleddem Smith dipped his words in sarcasm, "while I cope with this—this—"

"Hugger-mugger?"

A grin escaped the stern lines of the hero's mouth, briefly hinting at his father's sweetly endearing qualities, suggesting, perhaps, the man for whom Lady Sarah had surrendered girlhood dreams ten years before.

"He confers with our ferret," Aimée added.

"Yet our rabbit eludes him. Her survival tactics truly astound me."

"Unless someone helps her. you continue to assume the man driving her phaeton through Saint Kenelm is nothing more than a hired lackey." Aimée joined him at the window, where both could observe the huddle of hero-worshipers standing in a plane tree's shade. "In fact, he is probably her lover. I can almost hear them laughing at us."

"Enough!" He left her side to slump in one of the Sheraton armchairs. He would not tolerate her criticism.

"If my earl's daughter were to—," he swallowed, "to be unfaithful, I can assure you, it would not be with one who drives in public in his shirt sleeves."

"Hell's teeth! No one is as prim and proper as you want *her* to be!" Aimée waved through the window, the bright pink of her muslin gown obviously evident to the small crowd under the tree. "I presume when you questioned the ostler you were too arrogant to wheedle anything from him about who owned the phaeton."

"And I presume he would have remembered nothing—not even his name—so openly did you ogle him." Bleddem Smith returned fire.

171

"Well, I must marry someone, to give our babe an honest name!" She grinned at his indirect confession of jealousy and swayed over to the gold-framed mirror. "Surely, I can find someone willing to marry me."

Consumed with desire, Edward Bleddem Smith rested his elbow on an arm of the chair while shielding his eyes from her allure. Would he were in the midst of battle where there was far less strain!

She taunted him over her shoulder. "There's Captain Ashby or the Earl of Kettledene."

Bleddem Smith did not answer. What was he to do with a wife he no longer needed, and a woman he had to have. God! How Aimée could make him come alive! Her increasing girth was a constant reminder of his responsibility towards her . . . and the immortality won through descendants.

"At least we know you are not a widower." Aimée continued the study of her ample charms in the mirror. "A cuckold, perhaps, but not a widower." She pinched her cheeks. "And, at this moment, we can both be certain your son has no right to his father's name."

Under the shield of his hand, the war hero shook his head. He had been trained to make hard decisions, to demand sacrifices of the men in his command. It was time to exercise that training, before it withered. He arose and, from Aimée's shoulder, joined her admiration of the mirror's reflexion. He nuzzled through the sour smell of the thick auburn curls to nip at her earlobes.

"We will find a way to see the babe through an honourable birth. I swear."

Behind the gilt-encrusted door, they nestled on saffron brocade, undisturbed, for the remainder of the afternoon, desisting only when a cannonade of discord drew them out into the hall. Clearly, Emmaline Nimble's vehemence there outclassed Osmond Orr's smooth logic.

"You cannot let him stay out all night, Mr. Orr!"

"In here!" A grim Bleddem Smith ordered the adversaries into the salon, cutting off the supply of choice gossip for the footman in the reception hall below.

"Edward, dear. Mr. Orr has allowed Father the freedom to wander off. At this moment, he tells me, our father sits in the yard of The Bull and Mouth, checking every coach arrival in all the heat and the dust and the din. He could easily board one and be lost for ever."

"He's safe. Ferritt watches him."

"As he watched in the kitchen of The White Rose?" Bleddem Smith chose to remind the brawny retainer.

"I count on your father's habit to do what his memory can't—lead us to our runaway." Osmond Orr switched focus from the means to the end.

"But there is no coach till morning," Emmaline insisted. "Bring him home and take him back there tomorrow."

"Might interrupt his thoughts, and the nights have been comfortably warm lately."

"That's so," Aimée agreed.

"I see no harm coming to him." The sycophant drummed up a chuckle in support of his complaisant outlook.

"Or, you can simply wait for your wife to decide when she wants to return." He regarded his employer expectantly, knowingly.

"That might be best, Edward, dear. Less strain on all of us."

"No." The frigid blast informed Emmaline of how unwelcome her advice was as Bleddem Smith addressed his man of affairs. "Is it possible to leave this house unobserved?"

"Of course."

The war hero strode from the room without a backwards glance, the embodiment of decisive action. Treading lightly, Osmond Orr followed the icy trail. Though they *were* observed leaving the Grosvenor Square mansion, little was made of it. Thoughts of the evening repast occupied most people at this time of the afternoon, and enthusiasm over Bleddem Smith's heroics frayed at the edges. The ton had left for the country, of course, while the general populace turned to talk of the lottery, and the fifty-guinea prize for the race on Uxbridge Road.

In the tumult of the yard at The Bull and Mouth, the black-clothed figure of the little clergyman seemed an island of serenity as the men approached him from the rear.

"You see, he is perfectly content on the bench." Osmond Orr justified the new strategy.

Ferritt joined them. Between attempts to clear his nasal passages, he reported. "Hasn't moved since you left, Mr. Orr. Don't know as how he'll ever go any further towards choosing one particular coach."

"Father." The war hero stood behind his sire. "Which coach will take us to Sarah? Father?"

Bleddem Smith barely touched the frail shoulder, then moved to confront him. "Father?"

He crouched in front of the shadowed form and rested his hand on the bony knee. "Father," gently he called to awaken his sleeping parent without startling him. "Father."

The hero's voice caught. His hands turned cold. He had often witnessed death, but—No!

"Father," he pled. "I do remember when you saved me from drowning at Dog Falls."

Edward Bleddem Smith stood and straightened his shoulders, then looked about the booming transportation centre. Terrible, that his father should die in the midst of lumbering coaches and snorting horses, instead of in his quiet study or Sarah's garden at Long Wood. Bleddem Smith remembered her laughing insistence that his parents help plant the first rose bush there. Useless regrets, and even more useless memories.

In control again, the officer cleared his throat. "We shall have to develop another strategy for locating my wife."

"She'll doubtless come to the funeral," said a subdued Osmond Orr, not wanting to shirk responsibilities for even one minute. Not when they might lead to Aimée's best chance for a brilliant marriage, not to mention opportunities for graft beyond his wildest dreams, as aide to Bleddem Smith's rising star.

Edward Bleddem Smith's press of duty—and the not-to-be-neglected portrait sittings—kept him from accompanying his siblings and their families on Featherstone Smith's final journey north. Summer heat necessitated the prompt funeral.

Also, the hero had begun writing an account of his victory, since Aimée's epic poem had run aground on the poor rhyming potential for Napoleon and Bonaparte. To this end, His Majesty's obedient servant had appropriated an aerie on the mansion's top floor, where he could give his undivided attention to every detail of the event.

By late morning this day, Edward sat bare topped in the July heat that seemed to concentrate in the small cabinet. His discarded dressing robe of dark blue silk lay draped over the back of the plain wooden chair.

"Enter!" he answered the discrete knock at the door, adopting a look of annoyance, though secretly relieved at the interruption.

Osmond Orr complied. The buff and blue fabrics covering his weakening muscle structure, if not flattering, were exquisitely tailored. Plump fingers came together above the exaggerated cravat. He bounced them against his mouth in a pose of consummate reflexion.

"I hate to intrude, but your butler informs me there is a man has called and insists on seeing you."

"Everyone wants to see me." Pen in hand, the historian referred to the almost blank page in front of him. Two sentences had been scratched out.

"On matters concerning your wife."

"Ah." The officer's pale blue eyes locked with Orr's for a moment before fastening on the view of London rooftops outside the window.

"The name?"

"A Mr. Trimmer. Charles Trimmer."

"A familiar one." He frowned, trying to remember why. "I will see him."

Pushing his chair from the narrow writing table, Bleddem Smith donned his dressing robe. "And you will observe him without his seeing you."

If the fates were kind . . .

=19=

"Ah, yes. Trimmer. At Helder, wasn't it?" Bleddem Smith did not offer his hand, but indicated a chair opposite the door, which remained slightly ajar. "I remember you."

Charles Trimmer cocked his head at the implications in the last sentence while thoughts of past indiscretions raced in review. Just what did the hero remember?

"Who can ever forget all that rain?"

"Undoubtedly contributed to our lack of success against the Dutch."

A long pause followed this punctilious agreement on the weather during the botched attempt at invasion.

"As I recall, Trimmer, enough money, and no assignment is too petty nor too illicit for your notice." Bleddem Smith, standing guard at the door, backed against it.

The snap of its closing cracked like gunfire through the quiet library. Someone had spied on them from just behind that door. In the hostile silence, the dandy began to regret his demand for an audience. Here in the bowels of the mansion, a press gang could be summoned to carry him off and none the wiser.

"Your insult, sir, will cost you an additional ten pounds." The queasy feeling in Trimmer's gut receded, and he could relax against the padded leather back of the chair.

"My frank description of your past operations was not intended to insult, but to assist us in reaching immediate consideration of your business with me, free from the duplicity you may have planned."

How could he have forgotten! Trimmer shifted in his seat and gave thanks for present freedom from superior officers. Hell's fire! *His* was the advantage, what with all the talk about Bled 'Em Ned's search for a wife he could not find. There was money riding on the outcome, and sympathy for the wife among those with wagers.

"You have intelligence regarding my wife?"

"I have." The comely Charles, crossing one well-formed leg over the other, managed an *hauteur* equal to his host's.

"Well. What is it?"

"Have we settled on the price you pay for the information? Plus the aforementioned additional ten pounds." He was beginning to enjoy the interview.

"How can I judge its worth until I have heard it?" Bleddem Smith leaned against the door, arms folded over his chest. In the foreign robe of dark blue silk, he looked the potentate of some exotic realm.

Trimmer lost his advantage to the prolonged stare. "She was at Madden, with a face stained blue, on the twenty-seventh of June," he exploded, anxious to justify the importance of his visit. "Unable to pay her reckoning at the inn there."

"You believe I would give credence to such a preposterous account of Lady Sarah?"

"No. Until you conversed with Mr. Enos Harderbeck, the inn's proprietor."

"Madden?" The hero's frozen face showed signs of life.

"The spa."

"I have never heard of it."

"North, and east of Birmingham."

"Birmingham. South of Ludbury, then?"

"And west."

"At Madden."

"Madden." The dandy pulled at the front of his fawn-coloured coat and arranged each snow white cuff. "I understand she had been travelling with actors, which might explain the blue face."

"Actors!"

"Actors who, as they are wont, left her without funds. What she did to remedy her situation . . . we can only surmise. But she was not happy when I recognised her and she denied her identity." Trimmer's innuendos slithered into the fray. "One has to question if she supplements the allowance I assume you give her."

Bleddem Smith's hands gripped his upper arms in a vice that could have choked the life from a black-haired blackguard who dared such intimations. He still controlled the proceedings, however. "What were you doing in Madden?"

"I have the honour to bring the benefits of The Celestial Bed to every corner of the kingdom."

Bleddem Smith studied the crammed disorder of the shelves across from him. What did his earl's daughter do in such company? Had she lost her mind? "Is my wife still in Madden?"

"I believe she left that day for her home, by coach. She recovered from her financial embarrassment rather quickly, it would seem."

"She has not come home." The officer rubbed his forehead with one hand.

Trimmer shrugged, satisfied with his opponent's discomfort. "Perhaps a coaching accident."

"There have been none reported . . . Your business thrives in London?"

"No one is in town."

"No one, that is, to afford your prices."

Trimmer's graceful nod did not acknowledge the degree of business decline experienced since Madden. Whether it was the duration of the hot weather or Vesuvia's blue face, but laughing derision rather than awe had dogged his venture almost to London's outskirts.

He counted on Bleddem Smith's generosity to see him through lean times until The Celestial Bed was better established.

Another long silence threatened the business man's composure. He repeated adjustments to his modish attire and uncrossed his legs. Why were chairs designed only for the tall?

Just as he had lost all hope of a profitable encounter, Bleddem Smith began to parley.

"Your arrival this morning, Trimmer, is rather propitious." He stopped, unable, or unwilling, to continue. Hands behind his back, he looked away, allowing his visitor a profile view of the blond good looks. "We have been searching for Lady Sarah for almost a month now, and have reason to believe she has lost her senses. Some of these old families, you know. Eccentricity becomes madness before one realises it. Your report merely confirms our worst fears."

So that was the game. Call her dicked in the nob and bury her in some asylum, leaving the hero gloriously unhindered in his enjoyment of the auburn-haired cow.

"For her own good, we must find her, before she harms herself—or someone else. She could damage the nation's ability to check Napoleon's appetite for conquest."

How, in God's name, could Lady Sarah Smith accomplish that? Charles Trimmer's wide eyes conveyed his astonishment at the extravagant fiction.

Bleddem Smith unveiled his logic. "Unthinkable to have a mad woman dishonouring my name, if I am to have an expanded leadership role in the fight against tyranny. My experience could mean the difference between victory and defeat. We cannot afford another Helder campaign."

Trimmer nodded an understanding he did not own. Ill at ease with the conversation's direction, he had difficulty swallowing against his dry throat.

"If you were to start at Madden and find her, then re-

store her safely to me, I will recompense you, generously." The warrior gazed intently at the dandy. "And, addi-
tionally, eschew any mention to authorities of your
various infringements of the law."

Infringements of the law! He was a legitimate business
man, simply taking occasional advantage of careless
management on the part of others—cargoes redirected,
a few periods switched in inventory listings, and a rare
marked playing card along the way. Trimmer shifted in
his chair and swallowed again. Oh, for a drink! Even or-
geat would be welcome!

"Fifty pounds now and fifty when you return with Lady
Sarah. Should you accomplish our reunion within the
week, I shall add another fifty pounds to your total
remuneration."

Trimmer trifled with the onyx square decorating his
cravat. Foul play here. Still, one hundred—one hundred
fifty—pounds was difficult to ignore, what with Vesuvia
affecting the blue face and likely to run off with the first
man promising warmer climes.

"Agreed." The man *was* the husband, and had the right.

Bleddem Smith withdrew the bills from a cache within
the dark blue robe and placed them one by one on a small
table before moving to open the door.

"Use whatever means necessary to bring her back—
safely."

He led Trimmer to a rear portal and pointed across the
formal garden. "You will find it convenient to leave
through that side door in the garden wall. Send me word
when to meet you there. After dark."

"Where you will be waiting with the remaining one
hundred pounds in your hand."

With the merest nod, Bleddem Smith indicated intention to comply. From the shade of one of the arches
designed to support the first floor terrace, he watched
the handsome scoundrel cut across the garden's green
symmetry and disappear through the gate. Bleddem

Smith shook his head. To be forced to deal with one of such vile connexions was a heavy price paid, to maintain honour in the midst of fame's temptations.

Visions of Sarah crowded his mind's eye—her laughing face above a basket brimming with roses cut from Long Wood's garden. A gleeful Sarah, mud-spattered, holding a handful of slime that when cleaned would prove to be Roman coins. He remembered her tears when hopes that she was with child proved false.

His own tears, creeping towards the stern jawline, brought relief from the burden of his recollections. He was only doing what had to be done. His country needed him, and the babe needed his father's name.

"Aimée would have me remind you of your promise to take her for a carriage ride."

Osmond Orr's suave cheerfulness lapped this shaded shore of the garden. His presence startled the hero, who stepped away, preferring to keep his back towards his man of affairs.

"We have been looking for Sarah in the wrong part of the country."

"Impossible."

"He saw her in Madden. *South* and *west* of Ludbury."

"And he can lead us to her?"

"I have made it worth his while to locate her and escort her back," the officer replied coldly, studying the line of tall, narrow cypress trees marching in perfect order besides the back wall, reminding him of Mediterranean lands. "We must be prepared for their return."

"In what way?"

"Arrange for a long sea voyage. Somewhere from which return would be near impossible. Port Jackson in New South Wales comes to mind, for both of them."

His back still to Osmond Orr, Bleddem Smith did not see the flash of exasperation his scheme provoked from the flunky's usually amiable face.

"You will want the fellow watched, of course," Orr

prodded, "in the event our trust is misplaced."

With a detached gesture, the war hero signalled dissociation from attention to details. Sarah had always seen to them for him.

=20=

"STOOD THERE BY this great pile of luggage, calm as you please, as if they waited for their carriage in the middle of London."

Nothing of note had occurred in Derby W. Stout's constabulary since the peculiarity in the June twilight. Having inflicted his account on regulars at all the better public houses, he was reduced to seeking audiences at the lesser ones.

"Looking so out of place and all, of course, I thought they were spies."

In a corner of the rude tavern, Charles Trimmer paid no attention to the blather and bluster. He reached under his coat to relieve the itch along his ribs. Who knew what vermin had found a home on his person while he combed a countryside seemingly unaware of such benefits of civilisation as spotless bed linen, never mind a decent temperature for wine.

"What's more, she used French words."

The disgruntled Trimmer glanced at the group of rapt yokels before sipping again the warm brew in his chipped mug. He curled his lip at this blatant evidence of indifferent management and scratched under his wilted cravat.

Almost worse than the vermin was the incessant snuffling from his companion—the red-nosed rat sitting at the other end of the long trestle table. His presence had been a constant since Trimmer began his search at Madden four days ago. Unbelievable, the length Bleddem Smith would go to get his wife back. All that noble talk of victory over Napoleon, but Trimmer wondered if the great hero tired of his auburn-haired cow. And how much did he pay the sniffling rat?

The mistrust was mutual, and one hundred additional pounds, on delivery of the merchandise, had lost their lure for Trimmer. He should have asked for one thousand.

Laughter erupted from the group around the old fool in the ancient tricorn. Trimmer scowled, finding such revelry inappropriate for his morose state. Assuming he found Lady Sarah—and that assumption was rapidly losing validity in this land of the close-mouthed—how could he persuade her to accept his escort back to her husband?

The logistics of transporting an unwilling female bothered him. He would have to hire a coach, and a driver, more expence than he cared to incur. He drained the last drop from his mug and prepared to leave. Standing, he stopped to stare at the red-nosed rat.

"Never seen such a queer hat. A yard wide, at least, with big red circles dotted all over it."

Charles Trimmer turned from the door. That sounded like one of Vesuvia's wild creations—in fact, the one she claimed had been her masterpiece.

"With red trimming and a big red flower on the side." The narrator demonstrated.

There could not be *two* such hats in the world. Trimmer moved over to the edge of the little gathering.

"*And* a black face, mind you. She said it was blue, but it looked black to me. Well, I felt it my duty to take her to higher authority."

Blue face, under Vesuvia's spotted hat? It had to be Bled 'Em Ned's Lady Sarah. The hundred more pounds were as good as his! Trimmer spared a glance for his sniffling appendage, unconcernedly nursing his tankard. A louse would be better company.

"I knew Jack Rutland would know what to do. He always recognises when good men perform their sworn duty."

A murmur of agreement fortified the constable's opinion. "He said it was vigilance like mine that freed him from sleepless nights in these troublesome times." Derby W. Stout bobbed his head for emphasis.

"For certain, he's made something out of old Gaunt's acres," said one from the audience, who then turned to fill another's request for information. "Calls it Chance 'cause he won it."

Jack Rutland, a landowner, here? And as close-mouthed as the natives. It would be like him to shelter runaways and lost causes. But his presence changed things. Trimmer did not want Jack Rutland as an opponent. There was more behind that relaxed charm than charm, and Trimmer did not care to tangle with it.

Another burst of laughter interrupted his weighty calculations. Hell's teeth! He was a business man, not a villain, and knew when to cut his losses. Why not settle for the fifty pounds he already had . . . plus, perhaps, a little extra. Then, he could head back to London and a decent bath. He brushed at a smudge on the sleeve of his bottle green coat. There were always financial rewards in titillation, if he would just stick to his Celestial Bed scheme and be a little more patient.

"You!" Trimmer banged his end of the trestle table to gain the sniffler's attention. "I want to talk to your partner." There was always a partner, especially for one this inept. "Both of you be here in plain sight within the hour. I have some vital information I want to sell."

= 21 =

WORD CAME OF the dandy's departure and an end to all en-
quiries. The aging bear and the weasel, however, still
rooted around. Were they waiting for Bleddem Smith?
From descriptions, the pair sounded like his agents from
the skirmish at Ludbury. What clue had led them here in
the search for Sarah? Rutland scowled. He had thought
his torturous route from Ludbury impossible to follow.

"Ho, girl."

He reined in the prancing mare, snorting her objections to the easy cantre up the grade, and scanned the
approach to his major tenant's household. The early
morning sun gave sharp clarity to every stone in the
gabled block of farmhouse, granary, and stable. The pond
did not so much hold water as a million glistening drops.

Was it knowledge of menace behind the beauty that
allowed such keen perception? Rutland's eyes swept the
forested ridge to his left for any sign of movement. Or
did anticipation lend this appeal to the setting?

He had not had a close look at Lady Sarah Smith since
depositing her within the Pebbleships' warm welcome
immediately upon return from Ludbury. Prepared to
counter either force or slander, the master of Chance
restricted himself to salutes from a distance, until now,
when he needed the reassurance a new stratagem would
bring to a contest dependent on Bled 'Em Ned's affinity
for the thick of battle. When would the hero return to

war where he belonged?

"Jack Rutland." Andrew Pebbleship and his two eldest sons hailed their landlord. "You'll stay for breakfast."

Stable John, appointed bodyguard, dropped the harness he mended by the door leading from the kitchen and raced to hold the mare. "Sir!"

"Do you stay close to Mrs. Smith?"

"Ay." The seamed face exuded confidence. Labelled a knock-in-the-cradle soon after his birth on Gaunt lands, the ageless sprite flourished with the rest of the holdings under Rutland's leadership.

"You know where she is this minute?"

Stable John pointed back at his abandoned perch, where the lady in question now stood watching the young Pebbleship daughter advance on the visitor. The child capered about Rutland's long legs.

"Jack Rutland. Jack Rutland," she begged for his attention.

He obliged, bending to hand her the dark red campion fastened to his rough linen shirt.

Stable John pointed to the little girl's posy. "*F* is for *flower*." Pride compelled this display of benefits reaped from daily service as escort to and from the mill.

"*F* is for *flower*. *F* is for *flower*." The child skipped back to show off her prize to Lady Sarah, still in the doorway. "*F* is for *flower*, Mrs. Smith."

"How lovely, Jenny."

She was elegant, even in faded cotton dress culled from a Pebbleship trunk, and the homely touch of flour-smudged cheek. Lady Sarah bent to sniff the proffered blossom. Rising, she trapped Jack Rutland's admiring eyes with the shine in her own.

If the lady and gentleman thought their mutual esteem escaped notice, they missed the mark. Possibilities for their future enthralled the entire Pebbleship clan, as did Rutland's warning that the lady could be in peril. The sons especially embraced defence plans for every contingency. Lady Sarah still found it difficult to believe in their necessity, in spite of the action at Ludbury, but heeded Jack Rutland's precautions nonetheless.

"Come while it's hot," screeched Aunt Pitt, emerging from the house with her apron flapping. Of kinship so distant no one could remember the connexion, the tiny woman survived eighty years as a maiden lady in other people's homes by missing no opportunity to make herself useful. "Jack Rutland, do stay for breakfast, and I'll slice the last of the beef you brought us."

"Hard not to yield to your wiles, Aunt Pitt," Rutland drawled, trailing after the strays she sought to herd inside, "but I want a word with Mrs. Smith this morning."

A teasing grin for the spinster did not minimise the tender regard warming his face as he led Lady Sarah to the centre of the yard.

"Our Ludbury friends discover your haven here." His fingers brushed at the flour on her cheek.

"Oh." Lady Sarah shivered in the heat of the morning, hands clasped in front of a body becoming too thin. "Is my husband with them?"

"Not yet. I presume they alerted him and only await his arrival before making their move."

She sighed. It would be a relief, really, to confront Edward rather than endure any longer the threat of his hostility.

"I could not hide away for ever."

"No. but you can surround yourself with strong allies when negotiating for a truce."

"I hate to involve so many in my embarrassment."

"The embarrassment is his."

She shook her head, as if trying for the clear mind that would win exit from this maze. "If Edward and I could sit down together at Long Wood—just the two of us . . . "

"Ideal, of course. But do you imagine he could appear without entourage?"

"No."

"Here on Chance land, you and I and Andrew Pebbleship—reenforced with legal counsel—will demand of him the honourable behaviour he publicly endorses."

"With the cost of legal counsel falling on you and your ram." She could not contain frustration at being without money when in the past she had managed it for the Bleddem Smith household.

"A pittance." Rutland took her arm, leading her towards the access to the kitchen. "And the ram and I can look out for ourselves. We're pretty lusty fellows—at least, the ram is. I offer you every assurance, my lady, there will be money for your convenient kitchen—and a nursery far enough removed to relieve you from the children's clamor—when our house is finished."

She managed a wistful smile. "How perfectly you understand my basic concerns, Jack."

"You would find it easier to have faith in our ultimate victory, my Sarah, if you would eat more."

She shivered with delight at the pressure of his hand on her back as he saw her through the doorway. How wonderful it was, to be the object of his caring! She resolved to play the trencherman at breakfast.

Further recovery of Lady Sarah's spirits resulted from indisputable evidence that educational progress occurred at a mill awash in bright colours from Pebbleship paintbrushes. Not wanting to fuel Bibby Bibbrow's resentment, she limited her visits to the mill, but delivered on this day nine number cards which she herself had executed with surprisingly eye-catching results. In her honour, Belle led from the meadow to the mill a line of students reciting perfectly the entire alphabet. Lady Sarah had applauded until her hands hurt.

Still buoyant, she marched back to the farm chanting the alphabet with Walter Pebbleship and Stable John. Nothing discouraging could touch her while she kept time to the martial air.

Mr. Froggie Went a-Courting cheered them through the

brief darkness of the thicket beyond the packhorse bridge. *"The owl did hoot, the birds they sang, through the woods the music rang, mm-mm, mm-mm."*

Did they hear a horse nicker behind the web of brush and bramble? The vigour of their voices made it impossible to determine.

No matter. There was Jack Rutland, waving from the distant rise, looking for all the world like King Arthur promising return in troublesome times. The mare's chestnut coat gleamed in the sun.

Wildly, the trio waved back and began to deal with *The World Turned Upside Down* on the final ascent to the stony patchwork of ells that had accommodated ebbs and flows of Pebbleships over generations of working the land.

"If ponies rode men, and if grass ate the cows." They filled the summer air with nonsense. *"If mamas sold their babies to gypsies for half a crown . . . "*

During the afternoon lull in domestic industry, the senior Mrs. Pebbleship tested the waters of portraiture by the dim light of the front parlour's eastern exposure. Her replenished supply of paints offered the opportunity to paint a subject worthy of Gainsborough's brush.

"July's near over. Is Bibby Bibbrow persuaded to allow more teaching?" The plump little widow peered around her easel at the sitter: Lady Sarah, in the forget-me-not blue muslin and moonstones set in silver filigree.

Her ladyship, making every effort to hold still, answered with a shake of her head. She fidgeted in the hard chair without Aunt Pitt's lively conversation to help pass the time. The tiny spinster, hand spindle idle in her lap, had fallen asleep to the soporific drone from the kitchen, where Stable John arbitrated the children's constant wrangle over stemming the gooseberries. Lady Sarah, apprehension returning, nearly succumbed to the same drone. She caught herself wanting to check on her father-in-law before remembering he had left her care. A dog barked and stopped.

"It's your jewels." Mrs. Pebbleship sighed from behind the easel. "Difficult to capture their glow. They look no different from your eyes." Another check of the subject, and she disappeared to try again. "I have created a necklace of eyes." She groaned in dismay at her artistic shortcomings. "Oh, well. We can always use the painting at school. For the *E*'s."

Lady Sarah stirred in the chair. The discord from the back of the house heated up, and young Mrs. Pebbleship's voice entered the fray. A slight thump and a creak, and Lady Sarah looked at the door. Slowly it opened to reveal the dimensions of Osmond Orr.

"Lady Sarah." He spoke softly but amiably, closing the door behind him. "It's time we put an end to your estrangement."

She held tightly to the sides of the chair seat. "Yes. It is." She had forgotten the size of him, or had he never loomed so large when in a room with Edward? "But why does my husband not come himself?"

"He prepares to return to duty."

"Without saying good-bye?"

Still holding to the chair seat for dear life, Lady Sarah managed to duplicate Orr's civility through a mouth dry with anguish. The daring of him, to enter unannounced a bustling houseful of women and children! He had not even removed his hat!

"That's why I've come to take you to him."

"Where does he go?"

"I cannot say, but he is most anxious to settle things between you."

"As I am." She hesitated and rose from her chair, keeping a firm hold on its back. "I will get my things."

"Where's the need? We collected your baggage in Ludbury, from The White Rose. Best to leave immediately with a minimum of fuss." There was an edge now to his finesse.

"Nevertheless, Mr. Orr, I have a few things to gather,"

spoke the descendant of earls. "And I owe my hosts the courtesy of farewells. If you return in an hour, I shall be prepared to depart."

"Well, now, Lady Sarah. That just won't be possible." Orr advanced on her. "What with him leaving so soon. Even now, we may not make it in time. Took us a while to find you."

"Us?"

"Mr. Ferritt accompanies me."

"I think Bibby Bibbrow wants us to beg him on bended knee." Mrs. Pebbleship, with the advantage of deafness, remained unaware of the intruder. "I hate to give him that satisfaction, but you say the teaching succeeds."

"She has lost her hearing," Lady Sarah explained to her husband's man of affairs.

He jerked his head towards the door. "If we can be on our way."

Aunt Pitt's hand spindle rolled from her lap to the floor. She slept on, but the bump jarred Mrs. Pebbleship from her attempts at perfection. Noting the stranger in her parlour, she left the easel and extended her hand. "Welcome to our home."

Osmond Orr stared at her. The unexpected report of the falling spindle had jarred his extraordinarily thin urbanity. Quick to panic, he abandoned the guile which might have succeeded and reverted to the forceful practices of his youth.

"Unless you come now, Lady Sarah," he grabbed her arm, "I cannot answer for the consequences."

Iron grip on her arm notwithstanding, Lady Sarah raised her eyebrows and slowly repeated his words. "You cannot answer for the consequences! I cannot think my husband would countenance your tone of voice, Mr. Orr, nor—" she indicated his grip on her arm.

"You mustn't leave before refreshing yourself this warm day. Mrs. Smith, do go to the kitchen and tell them—," but it was too late for Mrs. Pebbleship's attempt at a ruse.

Fear over the passage of time in what had been planned as a hawk's swoop fed the aging bear's panic. One mighty cuff and he rendered Lady Sarah inert before carrying her from the room with surprising speed, through the front door and out to the red-nosed weasel astride one horse and holding reins of the other. Orr lifted his burden into Ferritt's limp arms.

"You rascal!" Mrs. Pebbleship had picked up the hand spindle to beat at Orr's retreating back and buttocks. "Help! Help!"

In the kitchen, young Mrs. Pebbleship reacted promptly. She shoved daughter Jenny up the stairs towards safety and bid Walter ride for help, almost before the abductors had disappeared into the wooded foothills separating the farm from Jack Rutland's river valley view to the south.

Stable John, wiry legs pounding over the ground, charged into the woods after them. He knew he could keep track of the riders as long as they used the rugged way through the trees, and he resolved not to fail in this most important hour of his sorry life.

Consciousness returned to Lady Sarah, head drooping, throbbing with each jolt from the horse's struggle over rough terrain. She opened her eyes and instantly closed them against bright sunlight dodging the evergreen trees.

Why head west? Was Edward there? Did he sanction— did he order this mistreatment? No! Please. Not her husband.

Jack! Help me! she called silently.

Snuffling in steady unison with the horse's hooves, the rider who held her coughed. She willed herself not to cringe when his spittle sprayed her neck. She would feign unconsciousness until she could surprise them with a dash to freedom . . . or until Jack came.

"Can't you ride faster?" Osmond Orr's impatience broke the quiet rhythm.

Lady Sarah peered through narrow slits of her barely opened eyes. He was enough ahead to be almost hidden by foliage. If she dropped to the ground now . . .

Her captor shifted his hold on her. "Not and carry dead weight, I can't." He kicked the flanks of his mount. "You must've really whacked her."

He did. Indeed he did, Lady Sarah mentally concurred. "She deserved it."

The pig! How could Edward choose such assistance? Tears of self-pity threatened the sham of unconsciousness she perpetrated. A pig, and *O.O.* stands for *oink, oink*! Unspoken defiance stemmed the lachrymal flow.

"We'll be forever reaching the coast at this rate."

"No need to go that far. No need at all." O.O. oiled his self-satisfaction.

Their horse drew closer to Orr's. "How will we send her to New South Wales if we don't reach the coast?"

New South Wales! Was Edward cruel enough to exile her from everything she held dear, or would he be with her there amidst the "alien corn"?

"We don't send her to New South Wales, Mr. Ferritt."

Ferritt, the snuffling man with the red nose in The White Rose kitchen, escorting her to limbo.

"Well, that's what we're supposed to do." Ferritt sniffed at a faster rate in the higher altitude.

"I have a better plan."

"I'll be grateful to hear it, I tell you. What with lugging this bag of bones on a rough ride." Ferritt slumped in his saddle, his slim form pressing upon Lady Sarah's back.

She suffered the insult and the pressure of his body in silence. When could she slip away?

"A little more patience, and we can ride off to London unencumbered, like gentlemen." Orr wallowed in the smugness that comes with the advantage of command. "Rising to the top of the heap, Mr. Ferritt. Me and Amy, with old Bled 'Em Ned pulling our wagon."

"No more left jabs and right punches."

"No more left jabs and right punches *received*. I'll still *give* a few, when necessary."

To women and children, doubtless. Lady Sarah dropped down farther against the arms that held her, putting more strain on Ferritt's ability to guide his horse.

Conversation ceased as both men sought the continued sure-footedness of their animals. Fewer trees blocked the sun during the climb towards a distant sound of rushing water. It grew cooler.

Never underestimate the opponent, Jack told her. She would concentrate on Jack's sagacity and be calm, but it was hard to think with a headache so intense. She grew nauseated. Did lilacs grow in New South Wales, like the ones Jack brought her that night in the kitchen?

"You're going to kill her, ain't you. Os?"

Osmond Orr gave no answer, but lengthened the distance between their horses.

Kill me! Lady Sarah's pounding hear must surely give her away. Pounding heart and pounding head. Involuntarily, she stirred in Ferritt's arms and moaned. She did not want to die. She had things to do with her life, muddled as it was.

Ferritt shifted her again. "You're going to kill her," he yelled at the back of Orr's disappearing figure. "Ain't you?"

Os halted and waited for the gap between them to close. "You want to yell a little louder? That way, everyone within fifty miles can hear you. Maybe come join our little outing." Ferritt had difficulty controlling both his steed and Lady Sarah's drooping body. "And I know who you plan to have do it." He did not lower his voice.

"It'll look like an accident," wheedled Os. "One long sweep of water, dropping clear to the bottom of the gorge ahead. All we have to do is toss her into the waterfall, and it does the rest. If she doesn't drown, she's smashed on the rocks." He paused, as if listening to the water's sound, closer now. "What could be simpler? And we can hardly be called murderers if we merely give her a chance to bathe." He chuckled over his logic.

Busy managing the tiring horses, neither man spoke. "Satisfied?" asked Osmond Orr, moving up on the path.

Ferritt followed. "What will the husband say to all this?"

"Not a damn thing. He wants her out of the way. He'll think she's at the end of the earth, as ordered. And who's to tell him different?"

Edward, who had thrilled her when she was seventeen, was indeed her enemy. Did he hate her that much? She hardly cared. She had begun to float in a space where her head did not ache. No need to worry, as long as she floated. She wanted to tell these men, and Edward, how contemptible she thought they were, but found it impossible to form the words from where she floated.

"Together, we toss her in the waterfall?" Ferritt requested confirmation.

"That's all."

"She'll put up a fight."

"An unconscious woman!"

"Not unconscious. Are you , Missus?"

A curve, and the way had widened just enough to allow them to ride abreast through outcroppings of grey rock. The distinct hum of plunging water signalled they closed in on Devil's Gorge.

A man waited here, almost indistinguishable from the rock on which he leaned. "I *am* sorry, gentlemen." He stood erect and slowly approached the dumbfounded miscreants. "This lady's not for killing."

Lady Sarah, through a feverish haze, saw the figure stalk her. Was this the one to try and kill her? With a last reserve of strength, she braced herself for fight or flight.

Jack Rutland walked—almost strolled—towards the

entrapped pair, having no wish to frighten them into further recklessness. Behind him, horses holding Stable John and the eldest Pebbleship son blocked further passage through the aisle of rock. There was not enough space to manoeuvre for purposes of retreat, even if Andrew Pebbleship and his second eldest offspring had not appeared on horseback to stand in the way.

"Don't touch me," howled a disoriented Lady Sarah, arms flailing, legs kicking, as she fell from Ferritt's horse into Rutland's outstretched arms. She pommelled his chest. "You'll have to kill me before I let you touch me again!"

"Hush, Mrs. Smith." Rutland's arms surrounded the wildly thrashing mass and held it firm against the warmth of his body until the ferocity subsided. "A fine welcome for a knight-errant," his lips whispered against the hot forehead.

"Jack?" Lady Sarah's voice was muffled, her head buried in the strength of his shoulder.

"Don't tell me you didn't recognise me."

She sighed, fervour spent. "I thought you had come to kill me."

"Not today."

=22=

A LONG NIGHT at Kettledene Court with the earl and Aimée as guttling companions had left Edward Bleddem Smith more than a little befuddled when he entered the splendid drawing-room where the Marlborough toothpick was displayed. He could see no one in the dark sea of gold brocade and squinted against the line of long, narrow windows, poorly placed to admit morning light. Visitors from London, the footman had said. The heroic officer knew of no immediate crisis to impinge upon his leave. Or was there an ever increasing need for his words of wisdom as well as his skill in weaponry?

"Yes?" He twisted an oval of black braid on his quilted robe around an errant button.

A slender figure moved into his line of vision and became recognisable. "Sarah!"

He stopped, almost in mid-stride, staggered by the miscalculation. Why did Orr bring her here? Surely he knew the importance of discretion. "You have been in London?"

"To determine your direction. A sorry thing, Edward, when a wife must enquire of strangers the whereabouts of her husband."

A wave of the war hero's hand dismissed her complaint. "Is Orr with you?" He turned to a second figure, barely discernible in the shadowed room. A male—not the physique of his man of affairs—lounged at the end of the glass case housing the earl's treasures.

"A distant kinsman of my family's." Lady Sarah anticipated her husband's next question with the scant identification she and Jack Rutland had contrived. "It is over his strong objections that I am here." She gulped for breath. "But I ran from your dishonour a month ago, Edward, so had to be the one to decry it now."

"Dishonour!"

"You are surprised. Surely you realise a broken vow—be it made to king and country or in a marriage ceremony—strips one of any claim to honour."

"You talk of two entirely different things, Sarah."

"I see no difference. Trust is trust, in every aspect of life. But if the word dishonour offends you, I can use traitor."

"I will not listen to this!" He protested to the shadowy male figure.

"There is another word for you Edward, even more applicable. Murderer."

"Murderer!" To make known his forbearance in the face of such exaggeration, the officer again looked to the other male in the room.

"Come, Edward. It is not like you to pretend innocence. When a man orders his wife's murder—"

"Sarah, you do not think—"

"No, Edward. I do not think you hatched murder. Merely ordered me sent, penniless and alone, to make my way in a strange land halfway around the world. As near a sentence of death for a woman as anything I know. But your man of affairs wanted it done quicker and planned to throw me off a cliff."

"I swear, if I had thought for one moment that your survival was at stake—"

"When you strut in the sewer, Edward, you must expect to acquire a stench."

"I had to do it, Sarah. For my son."

"Your son!"

"Soon to be born." How thin she was. Had Orr manhandled her? Infamous, if so. Bleddem Smith searched for those to blame. Too often he had been ill served. "Oh, Sarah. If only *you* could have given me this babe."

"How dare you hide behind my failure! How contemptuous!" She clasped her hands against her breast to still anger's assault on her body. Trembling controlled, she stumbled into recrimination. "Did our years of marriage count for nothing, then?" she asked, and immediately recognised the futility of such an enquery.

"They did. Of course." He noted the unfortunate state of her attire, a long mend in the forget-me-nots embroidered on a skirt hanging limp. Once, she had been a credit to him, always so beautifully turned out. "Understand, Sarah," he pled. "Hard decisions have been demanded of me for too long."

Lady Sarah sighed, the eloquence of righteous wrath spent. "I do not come to quarrel over the disintegration of our marriage, Edward, but to offer you the option of escaping criminal charges, should you want the name Bleddem Smith to stand through history for heroism in the defence of this nation."

"As it should, Sarah. Any legal battle would not become us."

"Nevertheless, I shall insist on your permanent exile from Britain."

"What do you mean!"

She turned, sending a silent appeal where Jack Rutland balanced, barely seated, on the edge of the long glass-topped box displaying curios. Though never doubting her resolve, he knew she neared the limits of her strength and entered the lists on her behalf.

"I speak for the Davess family, which believes Britain too small to hold you and any future hirelings you might engage to further dynastic ambition, not and allow Lady Sarah to thrive in good health."

Rutland folded his arms across his chest as he addressed the war hero, who stood as one carved in stone.

"Therefore, should you survive war service, seek assignments in the farthest colonies. New South Wales comes immediately to mind." Pleasantly, relentlessly, Rutland pressed on. "Futher hostile action against your wife, no matter how inconsequential, and I release to proper authorities the sworn statements from Orr and Ferritt, which I now have in my possession."

"I need no threats, sir, when honourable retreat is indicated."

"You can understand, though, how one might question this, after the past week's sad betrayal."

The nation's hero did not condescend agreement, but fortified the impassivity which enveloped him.

"In return for silence, the currently incarcerated Ferritt and Orr will be transported, rather than hanged by the neck until dead. How long they escape the hangman's noose in another land is moot."

Bleddem Smith gazed at his wife, as if memorising what he saw. "For some weeks, I have been thinking it was time to return to what I know best." He started towards his wife, but thought better of it when she flinched. "Sarah, good-bye." He moved swiftly towards the door.

"Edward.'

He turned back at her call.

"I will sell Long Wood."

"Do as you wish with the proceeds and any belongings you think I—might have wanted to keep. I leave the details to you."

The war hero departed the room. Its two remaining occupants stared at the rococo carvings on the door before turning to each other.

"How very unsatisfactory is retribution." Lady Sarah joined Jack Rutland at the case of curios. "And the role of aggrieved wife."

"Yes."

"Yet I remain his wife so long as we both shall live." Her eyes followed the trail of cherubs romping among scrolls on the plastered ceiling. "Actually, this is quite a suitable place for a marriage to lose all its meaning. There is not one natural thing in the entire apartment."

Rutland's eyes followed the same ornate trail. "We will not have such in our house."

"Not even the kitchen?" She flashed a wan smile.

"I suppose I could be persuaded, if your heart was set on it."

"I do not even know if I have a heart." She began to inspect the contents of Kettledene's glass-topped treasure chest.

"You have responsibility for two hearts now, Sarah."

"For interment at Long Wood."

She leaned down to read neatly inscribed labels by each relic before lifting the glass lid. Between the delicately formed lips of Bonnie Prince Charlie's ivory likeness she thrust the gold toothpick, and closed the case. An imperious tilt to her chin dared censure.

"Definitely adds some warmth to the decor."

"I thought so."

Rutland scanned the shadowed room. "Since we leave this a better place than when we arrived, shall we go? I want to collect your chaperon before she sees The Gold Kettle's sign and decides to paint a duplicate."

"She was snoring loudly when we left."

"Nevertheless, with Bibbrow's commission in her pocket, she may think a pot filled with gold worth his shilling and balk at accompanying you any farther."

"Not before my portrait is completed."

A footman, his black livery trimmed in enough gold to warrant a salute, saw them into their carriage. They did not spare even a backwards glance at the Earl of Kettledene's baroque extravagance as the carriage bore them towards the local inn.

"Did you have anything to do with Bibbrow's offer to

pay?" asked Lady Sarah, preferring to focus her attention on Mrs. Pebbleship's advance on fame and fortune.

"I thought it was you suggested it to him."

"I did. I never thought he would heed any advice I offered."

"He may surprise us all."

"Oh, Jack. I shall miss Chance."

"Of course. But Long Wood is merely the next stop on your progress, Sarah. I will not add 'to my bed' as it is inappropriate at this time."

"Dear long lost kinsman. How appropriate you are." Lady Sarah leaned her forehead against his shoulder, but immediately moved away from that comfort. "We both agreed. As long as I am married to Edward, I do not belong at Chance."

"I agreed. Just remember, you have not seen the last of me."

Early December

═══ 23 ═══

ANOTHER HOWL OF wind rattled window panes and ruffled papers on the floor of Long Wood's small morning room where Lady Sarah sat in the midst of organised disarray. "The wind thinks it March, not December," she commented.

Lady Toddington, mouth involved with a bite of sugared bun, could only nod agreement.

"I wish it *were* March, and winter behind us." Lady Sarah examined a small brass tray, burnished by firelight from the grate, before consigning it to the largest of three boxes.

"You discard Edward's smoking tray?" The visitor removed it from the box and set it under Edward Bleddem Smith's glove, which she had rescued earlier. "I say again, Sarah, you are acting too hastily."

"I know, Toddy." Lady Sarah took the last bun from the blue and white plate. "Do you remember how much my father-in-law loved these?" She bit into the sticky dough.

"No." The friend dismissed this old avenue of discussion. "When your world turns upside down, Sarah, you delay decisions until the right ones just seem to rise to the top. Like cream." Ever since returning from London with news of the reverend's death and Edward's departure, Sarah had closed her mind to the most carefully thought out suggestions. "Would Edward want you to sell his home?"

"Edward is dead, Toddy."

"I know, dear. I was here when the news came."

"I remember, Toddy."

From her sleeve, Lady Toddington extracted a handkerchief to dab her eyes. "You took it so bravely. Not one tear shed in public. Could not even bear to go to the funeral."

Sniffing, she restored to her sleeve the bit of fine linen, black bordered, the least she could do to honour him. She would not even comment on Sarah's merino dress. At least it was grey, but too flattering by far for one so newly widowed—Lady Toddington essayed a quick mental calculation— two months now since her noble neighbour was lost in battle. "Did your parents object to visiting such a disordered household?"

"They understand and want what is best for me."

Lady Toddington finished her sugar bun. "I thought they both looked well.'"

"My new venture encourages them to look towards the future."

"And have you decided yet exactly what your new venture involves, once the house is sold?"

"I still think on it, and that gives me pleasure, Toddy."

"It is too soon to dwell on pleasure, Sarah." Really an uphill battle, trying to impart her superior knowledge of how one should go on in times of grief.

"I know, Toddy, but please do not deny me this relief from responsibility."

Sympathy swept across Lady Toddington's aristocratic mien. "Dearest Sarah. Of course not. Harry warns me of my inclination to meddle," she confessed in a fit of contrition.

The door flew open, and a windblown young matron stormed in the room. "Good morning. Crippen said you were in here." She was tall, and not yet fat, though one could see she headed in that direction. Her dark brown riding outfit, gaping at the waist, was mud-daubed. "Oh. You have eaten all the buns. Crippen warned me."

"Kat! You rode over in this wind!" Lady Sarah clambered to her feet. "If the sugar buns are gone, there are mince tarts."

"No, no. Sit down, Sarah. Toddy." The newcomer sank on the sofa besides Lady Toddington. "I bring momentous news."

Attention assured, she volleyed. "Gib and I go to Jamaica. To see to his family's estates there. Sarah, you could come with us, for a long visit or a whole new life."

Lady Sarah, resettled on the floor, placed a stack of books, including Featherstone Smith's worn copy of *Robinson Crusoe*, into the largest box without thinking.

"Kat! You take my breath away."

"Good heaven, Kat. Before you think of visitors, you must consider the radical changes demanded by a life in the tropics." Lady Toddington spoke firmly. "Will you take a governess for the children? Do you buy clothes here or there? Have you ample supplies of cinchona bark to treat fevers?"

A chastened Kat seemed to pay such close attention to her friend's counsel, the latter directed all further advice towards this more open mind. Lady Sarah continued to sort household belongings during the lengthy oration on Jamaican life and customs, then, wrapping herself in an old woollen cape of faded burgundy, escorted her morning callers through the wind's bite to the edge of the long, narrow woods where their respective properties converged.

Face into the bluster, she inhaled the smell of the sea as she watched her friends disappear from sight, and turned towards home feeling at one with frenzied saplings whipped by the gale force.

"Halloo," she yelled, and raised her arms as if to embrace the wild elements.

She had been sitting by the hearth, doing as she ought,

for four months. Dismantling one life, speculating on a new one. Wondering if, in her vulnerable state last July, she had responded to Jack Rutland's kindness or to Jack Rutland. His image was fading from her mind's eye, and she questioned whether she could recognise him in a crowd.

She smiled, remembering her one message from the master of Chance—a hastily sketched, but sturdy *R*, on the reverse of which had been scrawled "is for *Rutland*" in a bold hand. A carter had delivered it not many days after grim-faced officers brought word of Edward's death in gallant action against the enemy.

Lady Sarah burrowed deeper into the old cape to counter the wind's attack on her shoulders and plowed through piles of leaves too wet from all the rain to fly from her scuffing feet. Edward, killed in battle, he who once had so much, in the end commanded only reckless courage. And she had felt nothing, not even the pity held for some stranger's death. She had become heartless and as cold as the wind. She shivered and looked up. Jack Rutland stood there, waiting for her. Not sixty feet away. Hatless, relaxed. His hands—oh, how well she remembered the look of his hands—resting at the base of his hips.

"Jack!"

She raced over the distance between them, the wind driving her forwards, to hurl herself on his solid frame. "Jack!"

Arms around his neck pulled his face within range of kisses scattered on his chin, his mouth, his cheeks. "Jack."

His arms tightened their hold on her, pressing her into the smooth surface of his woolen coat. "And I am glad to see you, too."

They stood together, without moving. Their closely touching bodies formed an island in the windswept world. Lovingly, Rutland rubbed his chin over the top of her head.

"How long do you want us to stay out in this windstorm?"

"For ever," Lady Sarah asserted from the warm cocoon between his arms and steady heartbeat.

He pulled his head back to study the features of her face, the grey eyes. "You have put meat on your bones. I can feel it." Lightly he kissed each cheek. "And fuller cheeks." He touched his lips to hers. "And lips. You no longer suit the role of grieving widow."

Free, now, to envision a life shared with him, Lady Sarah could truly comprehend all that he had come to mean to her, and was too overwhelmed to do anything but nod confirmation of this assessment.

"Then fill the role of my beloved wife."

Grey eyes met slate blue ones in solemn covenant. Then a gleam sparked the ones, and a glint filled the others.

"Would this be another of our strictly business arrangements?" asked Lady Sarah.

"Not this time."

The wind shrieked at the absurdity, and carried the laughter of the lovers in the direction of Chance.

THE END

If you have enjoyed this book and would like to receive details of other Walker Regency romances, please write to:

Regency Editor
Walker and Company
720 Fifth Avenue
New York, NY 10019